Vintage Dress Shop on the Island

De-ann Black

Text copyright © 2023 by De-ann Black
Cover Design & Illustration © 2023 by De-ann Black

All rights reserved.
No part of this book may be used or reproduced in any manner whatsoever without the written consent of the author.

This is a work of fiction. Names, characters, places, and incidents are either products of the author's imagination or are used fictitiously. Any resemblance to actual persons, living or dead, businesses, companies, events, or locales is entirely coincidental.

Paperback edition published 2023

Vintage Dress Shop on the Island

ISBN: 9798868017308

Vintage Dress Shop on the Island is the third book in the Scottish Highlands & Island Romance series.

1. Scottish Island Knitting Bee
2. Scottish Island Fairytale Castle
3. Vintage Dress Shop on the Island
4. Fairytale Christmas on the Island

Also by De-ann Black (Romance, Action/Thrillers & Children's books). See her Amazon Author page or website for further details about her books, screenplays, illustrations and artwork. www.De-annBlack.com

Action/Thrillers:
Knight in Miami.
Agency Agenda.
Love Him Forever.
Someone Worse.
Electric Shadows.
The Strife of Riley.
Shadows of Murder.

Romance:
Christmas Weddings
Fairytale Christmas on the Island
The Cure for Love at Christmas
Vintage Dress Shop on the Island
Scottish Island Fairytale Castle
Scottish Loch Summer Romance
Scottish Island Knitting Bee
Sewing & Mending Cottage
Knitting Shop by the Sea
Colouring Book Cottage
Knitting Cottage
Oops! I'm the Paparazzi, Again
The Bitch-Proof Wedding
Embroidery Cottage
The Dressmaker's Cottage
The Sewing Shop
Heather Park
The Tea Shop by the Sea
The Bookshop by the Seaside
The Sewing Bee
The Quilting Bee

Snow Bells Wedding
Snow Bells Christmas
Summer Sewing Bee
The Chocolatier's Cottage
Christmas Cake Chateau
The Beemaster's Cottage
The Sewing Bee By The Sea
The Flower Hunter's Cottage
The Christmas Knitting Bee
The Sewing Bee & Afternoon Tea
Shed In The City
The Bakery By The Seaside
The Christmas Chocolatier
The Christmas Tea Shop & Bakery
The Bitch-Proof Suit

Colouring books:
Summer Nature. Flower Nature. Summer Garden. Spring Garden. Autumn Garden. Sea Dream. Festive Christmas. Christmas Garden. Flower Bee. Wild Garden. Flower Hunter. Stargazer Space. Christmas Theme. Faerie Garden Spring. Scottish Garden Seasons. Bee Garden.

Embroidery books:
Floral Garden Embroidery Patterns
Floral Spring Embroidery Patterns
Christmas & Winter Embroidery Patterns
Floral Nature Embroidery Designs
Scottish Garden Embroidery Designs

Contents

Chapter One	1
Chapter Two	15
Chapter Three	28
Chapter Four	43
Chapter Five	56
Chapter Six	69
Chapter Seven	83
Chapter Eight	97
Chapter Nine	113
Chapter Ten	125
Chapter Eleven	135
Chapter Twelve	148
About De-ann Black	168

CHAPTER ONE

'We're in the magazine!' Skye came running into the shop to tell her sister Holly the news. She'd popped out of their shop to pick up fresh milk for their morning tea from the grocers and saw that the latest issue of the popular monthly fashion magazine was on sale. Two copies were now in her hands like winner's batons.

Skye was in her late twenties. She wore a fifties tea dress and her strawberry blonde hair was pinned up in messy pleats. Her blue eyes were wide with excitement.

'Let me see,' Holly said eagerly. She'd been arranging the front window display, putting pre–loved forties and fifties tea dresses on the three mannequins. Two wore pink and blue daisy print dresses, while the third was made from fabric printed with a tea dress design. Early autumn sunlight streamed in the window, casting a glow over the rails of vintage dresses hanging in the pretty shop.

Holly, early thirties, wore low heel, t–bar shoes with her autumn floral print forties dress that suited her chestnut hair and green eyes. She stepped out of the window, keen to see the magazine.

They owned the shop on the main street down by the harbour on a beautiful island off the west coast of Scotland. Barely twenty miles from the mainland, the nearest city was Glasgow, accessed by the regular ferry.

Lots of quaint shops were situated along the main street and wrapped themselves around the curve of the bay. Their shop was a traditional converted cottage with a storeroom and kitchen at the back. It was next door to Brodrick's cafe bar, and near Innis' cake shop, the tea shop owned by Lyle that was currently being refurbished, their friend Ailsa's craft shop, and the knitting shop where they attended evenings at the knitting bee. The lovely mix of shops along the main street added to the picturesque quality of the island.

A deep, blue–green sea surrounded the island, and the sandy coves were popular with locals and tourists, especially in the summer months when people enjoyed swimming in the sea and sailing around the island. Outlying islands on the far side helped protect the island from harsh winters, and the weather tended to be temperate, with snow falling only during the heart of winter.

White Christmases were guaranteed, as were bright winter days when the lush green and heather covered hills rising up from the coast sparkled with snow and ice.

Picture postcard Christmases and winters were equalled in their beauty by gorgeous autumns when the extended summers refused to go quietly. Golden hue days when the vibrant evergreen trees in the forest were offset by the burnished gold and bronze leaves of the other trees and foliage of autumn.

The forest surrounded the island's fairytale castle set within its own estate that included thistle loch, a silvery river and the enchanting forget–me–not waterfall. The magnificent castle was run as a hotel, catering for guests and special events such as weddings and other celebratory parties. Ceilidh nights and dancing were held regularly in the beautiful family–owned castle. The laird and his wife were away a lot on business and leisure time to the mainland, leaving their three sons, Finlay the laird to be, Innis and Ean, to run the castle and the estate. They lived in the castle and were happy to run it as a popular hotel.

Farms and cottages dotted the landscape and thrived as an island community with easy links to the mainland via the ferry.

Holly and Skye had trained in fashion and design on the mainland. They'd worked in fashion, taking part in fashion shows in the cities, but every time they visited their parents on the island, they wanted to move home, and now lived there with their parents. Growing up, their father's work had taken them to various parts of Scotland, including a brief spell on the isle of Skye where Skye got her name, but then they'd set up home in Dundee and Holly and Skye went to school there. But finally, they'd returned to their original home island.

Holly and Skye recently inherited the shop from their mother when she retired to enjoy more leisure time with their father. Their mother had inherited the shop from their grandmother, and now they were happy to take it on.

They loved vintage fashion and decided to continue to sell vintage clothes rather than high fashion. But they'd had a new sign with their names put up over the one their mother had. A few years before retiring she'd had a lovely sign put up — *the vintage dress shop*. Recently they wished they'd kept the original sign as it suited their business better than the vintage fashion boutique and their names, especially as sales of their dresses were so popular. Although they sold their dresses to local customers and holidaymakers and visitors to the island, the shop was selling more online than ever. Their website featured the dresses and a few other items like vintage skirts, tops and accessories, and their online customers often made repeat orders, so they were steadily building their business, especially sales of the dresses.

Over the years, their mother had built up numerous contacts supplying vintage dresses and gave this list of contacts to Holly and Skye. Often the dresses were sold in bargain bulk buys, enabling Holly and Skye to then sell the dresses in their shop as real bargains for the quality.

There was the added benefit that Skye and Holly loved sewing and mending. Skye's pink sewing machine was set up in the shop behind the counter. They were skilled at making any repairs needed to the dresses before selling them. This included invisible mending whereby the repairs were barely seen, to visible mending where the stitches were part of the design and enhanced the styling. Embroidering floral motifs on the dresses was something they enjoyed doing and the embroidery work was loved by their customers.

In the magazine, they were pictured wearing two of the vintage evening dresses while standing in front of their shop with the three mannequins in the window displaying pre–loved tea dresses.

Skye handed Holly a copy of the magazine. 'I bought two.'

Holly flicked through the pages until she came to their feature that had been photographed earlier in the year in the late spring. 'Wow! Look at our shop. It looks great and they've included the photos of us standing outside it wearing the vintage evening dresses.'

Skye's dress was oyster satin, and skimmed the slender curves of her model–like figure, with the front split revealing the length of her long legs. Pearly beige classic heels suited the thirties style dress. Posing in the sunlight, her long, strawberry blonde hair hung in shiny waves around her shoulders.

Holly was pictured modelling a pale blue silk evening dress, cut on the bias, and perfect for her slender figure. Her chestnut hair shone in the sunlight.

'It's so exciting.' Skye expected that the feature would look nice, but seeing the amount of space they'd been given in the fashion magazine, and the story about them and their wonderful vintage dresses was amazing.

And then Skye blinked, turning the page over where their feature extended, and gazed at the gorgeous looking man standing with her in one of the pictures. And other pictures of him, including a sizzling, hot close–up of him on his own.

Holly saw him too.

They paused and looked at each other.

'We did ask Innis if he wanted to be in the photos,' said Skye unconvincingly. 'I gave him copies for his website. He knew we were taking the pictures for the feature in the magazine.'

Holly bit her lip.

Innis owned the cake shop nearby. Additionally, he was one of the three, rich and handsome brothers living in the island's fairytale castle.

'Do you think Innis will see the fun side of this?' Skye said, knowing the answer.

'Nooo.'

'They're really flattering photos of him,' said Skye. This was true. Innis was one of the most handsome men on the island. Tall, fit, thirty–two, with dark hair, a brooding nature and amber eyes that had given him the reputation of having wolf eyes. He was known to be a wolf in wolf's clothing, a man who suffered fools badly.

'*Extremely flattering*. That's the problem. They've sort of slanted the feature a wee bit and made him look like he's....' Holly searched for a polite phrase and found none.

'Hot and handsome,' Skye suggested.

They both nodded and burst out giggling.

Innis wore a crisp white shirt with short sleeves that displayed the lean muscles in his arms to full effect. Black trousers showed his long legs, slim hips and taut torso. Innis baked cakes, but he specialised as a chocolatier, and wearing the shirt and trousers he looked the epitome of an artisan chef. A sexy one. In addition to the picture of him with Skye, and a full–length one of him standing looking like he belonged on the cover of a fashion or film magazine, there was a close–up of his handsome face with those amber eyes of his gazing straight at the camera.

'Scorching hot,' said Holly. She hadn't been tempted to consider dating Innis, but seeing him in the magazine, her heart reacted to his raw masculinity.

'Innis looks totally gorgeous.' Skye had considered what it would be like to date a man like him, and had decided he probably wouldn't be interested in her fashion work, and therefore not the man for her. She wanted a relationship like her parents had — a loving couple and great friends too. But looking at Innis in the magazine, Skye felt her resolve wane. Maybe if Innis ever, by some wild fluke, asked her out on a date, she doubted the words *no thank you* would drift from her lips.

'Hide!' Holly shouted, seeing Innis drive up and park outside his cake shop.

They peered through the window, hoping he wouldn't see them.

'Does he look grumpy?' Skye felt the need to whisper even though he couldn't hear them.

'No more than usual. Though I don't think he knows he's in the magazine.'

'What makes you think that?' Skye wondered.

'Because he's not making a beeline for our shop,' Holly surmised. 'But we'll have to deal with him later.' Her phone was lighting up with calls.

Alerts started pinging on their phones, indicating sales on their website along with customers contacting them.

Holly glanced at Skye, still clutching the magazine. 'I think we're going to be busy.'

'And a little bit famous,' Skye added hopefully. The whole point of taking part in the magazine feature in the spring was so that when the magazine came out in the autumn, it would help to promote their shop. She glanced at the orders and contact alerts popping up on the computer on the front counter. Her heart beat with excitement and slight trepidation.

'You check the online orders,' said Holly. 'I'll take the phone calls.'

Skye nodded firmly.

The magazine fashion feature was wonderful, and was sure to gain them publicity. And their shop had been featured in a Glasgow newspaper's magazine–style supplement recently, that had brought quite a bit of extra business their way.

And something was being highlighted — the most popular pre–loved clothes they sold were the vintage dresses, especially the classic tea dresses and elegant evening dresses.

Ailsa, their friend, owner of the nearby craft shop, walked past the window.

Skye waved out to her, beckoning her urgently to come in.

Ailsa hurried in.

'We're in the fashion magazine,' Skye told her and gave her the short course of the situation.

Ailsa was one of the most beautiful women on the island, and there were a fair few, including Skye and Holly. But Ailsa was a classic beauty, thirty, with slender curves, long legs, dark hair that tipped the top of her shoulders, a lovely pale complexion and azure blue eyes. In addition to running her own craft shop, she modelled knitwear and fashion, using her modelling work to boost her income while she built up her craft shop. She was born and raised on the island and had no plans to ever leave it. Her modelling work took her to various places on the mainland, so she was well–travelled, but she couldn't imagine anywhere better for her than the beautiful island in Scotland.

'The magazine feature is fantastic,' Ailsa enthused.

The three of them shared an excited hug, and then they asked for her help to deal with Innis.

'We don't think Innis knows yet that he's pictured in the magazine,' Holly told Ailsa. 'And we wondered if you'd phone Ean at the castle so he can tell him. Ean's such a sweetheart, and he adores you, so he's bound to want to help if you ask him.'

Ailsa hesitated, but knew it was best to phone Ean. She took a deep breath and called the castle.

'I think the castle and the gardens look lovely during the summer,' said Ean, admiring the view as he sat outside on the patio at the back of the castle having breakfast with his brother, Finlay. 'But autumn is probably my favourite time of the year. I'm thinking of painting it. I'll need more watercolour paints, so later I'll head down to the art shop in the main street to buy some.'

Finlay ate his cooked breakfast, tucking in, getting fuel for the hectic day ahead. Guests were leaving and more guests were arriving. Non–stop business all day, and there was a dinner party in the evening.

'An autumn painting would be ideal. And I have to say I liked you winter watercolours. Winter when everything's iced with snow might be my favourite time.'

Finlay was classically handsome, thirty–three, with thick blond hair, light aquamarine blue eyes, and a tall, strong, lean stature. He was the spit of his father, the laird, a very handsome man, and in line to take on the role of laird when his father eventually retired. Finlay's large white yacht, anchored down at the harbour, was his pride and joy. As an accomplished yachtsman, he loved to go sailing around the island's deep waters and further afield.

At thirty, Ean was the youngest of the three brothers, and inherited his auburn hair and green eyes from his mother. He was as tall and lean as Finlay, if perhaps a little less strapping, and a keen hill runner. This kept him fit and his muscles lithe. He owned a small boat, but art, painting watercolours, mainly occupied his leisure time along with the running.

The brothers were always well–dressed, wearing classic suits, expensive casuals in neutral tones, or their black and dark grey tartan kilted attire.

This morning, Finlay wore light beige and white casuals, while Ean opted for a white shirt, unbuttoned at the neck, and a pair of dark trousers, part of a suit.

Ean poured milk on his porridge and nodded, glancing up at the dark stone castle. 'Winter really makes it look like the fairytale castle folk talk about.'

They continued to chat about their plans for the day while finishing their breakfast, making the most of the warmth of the early autumn sun. The summer often lingered well into the later months, blending with the golden glow of autumn, creating months when the weather was at its best for those on holiday to the island and staying at the castle.

'Can I speak to Ean please? It's Ailsa,' she said to Geneen at reception.

Geneen knew Ailsa, Holly and Skye. They were all members of the local knitting bee and good friends. Geneen was in her fifties, a trim and efficient member of the castle's staff.

'Hold on,' said Geneen. 'Ean's having breakfast out on the patio with Finlay. I'll go and get him.'

Geneen hurried through to the patio at the rear of the castle.

'Sorry to disturb you, Ean, but Ailsa is on the phone for you. She called reception. She doesn't have your private number. She sounds a wee bitty keyed up.'

Ean sparked into action, throwing down his napkin. Delighted to have a call from Ailsa, as he'd long had a crush on her, he was equally concerned that something had to be wrong if she was calling him at the castle. She never phoned him. This would be the first time.

Running through to reception, he picked up the phone. 'Ailsa, are you okay?'

'Yes, fine, everything's fine, it's just that... You know that feature Holly and Skye took photos for earlier in the year? Around the late spring? They were interviewed for a fashion magazine and asked to provide pictures.'

'Yes,' said Ean. 'Skye and Holly were being featured in a fashion magazine and supplied photos of their dresses to go with it. Innis was encouraged to join them. He was only in a few. Skye gave him copies for his website. He put some up, but they were taken outside his cake shop to promote his fondant cakes and chocolates.'

'Well, the feature in is the latest issue of the magazine. It's on sale in the grocers. He ordered a load of extra copies because he knew local folk would be interested in reading it,' Ailsa explained.

'Yes, people love a local interest feature. We'll get copies for our guests at the castle,' said Ean.

'The thing is...Innis is included in the pictures.'

There was a pause. 'Innis is in the magazine?'

'Yes, and the pictures of him are very flattering. *Extremely flattering.*'

'Ah, right.' Ean started to understand the predicament.

'Someone will have to tell Innis,' Ailsa hinted.

'He left the castle to start work in his cake shop. I'll pop down and have a word with him. Can I pick up a copy of the magazine from you so I can see it before I tell him?'

'Yes, I'm at Holly and Skye's shop,' said Ailsa.

'I'm on my way. I'll be there in five minutes.'

Ailsa clicked the call off. 'Ean is coming to the rescue.'

'Phew!' Skye sighed. 'Innis will be okay once Ean explains.'

Ailsa, Holly and Skye glanced at each other, none of them entirely convinced about this.

'Innis will maybe go in the cream puff for a wee while,' said Ailsa. 'But then another drama will take over. There's the fashion show next week at the castle. We'll all be busy with that.'

'We've the meeting tonight at the castle to discuss Murdo making the runway,' Holly reminded her.

Murdo was a key worker at the castle, a sturdy man in his fifties, a handyman and builder and one of the castle's main assistants.

Ailsa had agreed to go with Skye and Holly to the meeting, combining their experience in fashion work.

While they were talking, Ean pulled up and jumped out of his car. But as he strode towards Holly and Skye's shop, Rory made a light–hearted comment to him.

Rory, tall, late twenties, was a local builder and helping convert his cousin Lyle's tea shop, building the upstairs level. Rory's van was parked outside the tea shop. The building work was almost done. He'd only a cupboard door to finish, and had popped out to his van for an extra piece of wood when he saw Ean.

'Tell your brother Innis he's got another career in the bag, as a male model, if his cake shop business ever nosedives.' He'd heard the gossip in the grocers and had a peek at the magazine there.

'Tell him yourself, Rory. Innis is in his cake shop,' Ean told him. 'It'll be better coming from you than me. You know what Innis is like.'

Rory started to back down. He knew the reputation Innis had for not suffering fools. 'I was just kidding.' He shrugged aside his jibe with a wary smile. 'Nice day we're having.'

'It is,' Ean agreed, and then walked on and went into Holly and Skye's shop.

He smiled at Ailsa, feeling his heart react. She was so beautiful. But he needed to see the magazine and decide how to tell Innis he was in it.

'Thanks for coming down.' Ailsa showed him the pictures.

'We did ask Innis' permission,' said Skye. 'But we had no idea that they'd make him look so...'

'Handsome,' Ailsa said, filling the awkward gap. 'But all three of you are the most handsome men on the island. Innis, Finlay and you.'

Ean was in turmoil. Part of him wanted to deal with Innis's situation. Clearly the magazine had over–egged the pudding and made his brother look rather sexy. On the flip side, which was winning, hearing Ailsa say that they were the most handsome men on the island, made him hopeful that if he asked her out on a date, a proper date, she'd accept. But now was not the time to ask her. Or was it? There was never a good time to even talk to Ailsa. Either he was busy with work at the castle, or on the mainland dealing with castle business. Or Ailsa was busy with her craft shop, or away modelling, something she'd done a lot of recently. He'd hardly seen her.

Lost in his thoughts, Ean blinked, realising Ailsa, Skye and Holly were looking at him, urging him to go and talk to Innis.

'I'll pop along to the cake shop and explain things to Innis,' Ean said, clasping the copy of the magazine.

Ailsa smiled at him. 'Let us know what he says.'

'I will.' Ean then left and headed to the cake shop.

CHAPTER TWO

The flower baskets hanging outside the yellow and pink exterior of Innis' cake shop were filled with colourful blooms, and the sun had quite a bit of heat to it.

Ean went inside and spoke to Rosabel and Primrose. They were working behind the front counter, wrapping cakes and dealing with customers. Wearing pastel pink and pale yellow respectively, they'd come out of retirement to work for Innis and share some of their family's secret recipes with him. They thought it was better for the recipes to be made into cakes for customers to enjoy rather than languish in a handwritten old notepad hidden away in a cupboard.

'I need a few minutes to talk to Innis,' Ean said to them, heading to the kitchen at the back of the shop. His tone indicated that he needed privacy.

'Yes, of course,' said Rosabel. They knew Ean well. He rarely disturbed Innis when he was baking, so they surmised it was something urgent.

Innis was icing a wedding cake when Ean walked into the kitchen. He glanced up, wondering if something was wrong.

'You're in the fashion magazine along with Skye and Holly,' Ean came right out and told him, and laid the magazine down on a table open at the pages showing the feature.

Innis wiped icing sugar from his hands and lifted up the magazine, scanning the editorial and studying the pictures.

'Ailsa told me. She's in Holly and Skye's shop. They're worried about your reaction,' Ean explained. 'Skye insists she didn't deliberately include your photos, but she must've sent everything they'd snapped that day, and unfortunately your pictures have been selected as part of the magazine feature.'

Innis frowned. 'They've made me look...'

'Like a male model,' Ean suggested. 'I mean, it's not as if you look bad, quite the opposite. But the ladies are concerned that you'll blame them. And it's really not their fault. They're so excited about the dress shop being featured.'

Innis nodded thoughtfully. 'Tell them I'm fine about it. Not entirely fine, but...'

'Thanks. Ailsa is trying to help her friends. She phoned me at the castle—'

'Ailsa phoned you?'

Ean tried not to smile. 'Yes, she asked for my help to tell you about the magazine feature.'

'Are you going to ask her out on a date?'

'I'm thinking about it. Maybe I could ask her to be my partner for the party after the fashion show.'

'You should do that. I know you like her,' said Innis, putting aside his own drama to concentrate on his brother's feelings for Ailsa.

'I told them I'd go back to the dress shop and tell them your reaction,' Ean explained.

'Tell them it's okay. And ask Ailsa for a date.'

Ean smiled. 'Thanks, Innis.'

Innis nodded, and then Ean hurried out of the kitchen.

From the looks on Rosabel and Primrose's faces, they'd now heard about the magazine feature, but they didn't say anything as Ean walked by and merely smiled and nodded to him.

Ean went back into the dress shop. 'Innis says it's okay. He's not thrilled, obviously, but it's fine.'

'Phew!' said Skye.

Holly looked relieved.

Ailsa stepped close and smiled at him. 'Thanks for your help. I know that I threw you in at the deep end, but...' she shrugged.

'You can always call me,' Ean assured her. 'And eh, I was wondering—'

The shop door burst open and Elspeth from the knitting shop hurried in. 'I heard you're in the magazine. Can I have a look?'

Primrose joined them, and soon the women were bustling around reading the feature and chatting about the pictures.

Ean smiled at Ailsa and left them to it. He'd ask her another time when she wasn't so busy.

Waving, he left the shop, but was surprised when Ailsa hurried after him.

'Ean! Wait. What were you wondering?' she said to him.

He smiled at her, feeling slightly nervous. She looked so beautiful standing there in the sunlight. The artist in him thought her eyes really were the perfect shade of azure blue.

'Did you want something from my craft shop?' The innocence in her eyes took him aback. 'I've got new watercolour paints in if that's what you need.'

He nodded firmly, remembering he'd mentioned about his art supplies when they were dancing at an event at the castle. Not as a couple, but as part of the party. 'That's exactly what I need,' he said, though he'd intended going to the art shop to buy them. 'I'm thinking about painting the castle in autumn, so I'll need more paint for that.' This part was true.

Ailsa dug the craft shop key from her bag and held it up. 'I ordered in top quality watercolour paints, professional artist quality, but if they're not what you want, you'll probably find them in the art shop.'

'I'm sure you'll have what I want,' Ean said, walking along with her to her craft shop. Ailsa was quite tall, but Ean towered over her. Lean and fit from his hill running, he cut quite an impressive figure. 'How did your modelling work go? You've been away a lot recently.'

'Wonderful. It's handy money and I enjoy modelling the knitwear and fashions. But I'm always glad to be back home.' She opened the craft shop door and they stepped inside. 'I feel I've hardly seen you lately.'

'Ships that pass in the night.' He looked around the shop with its eclectic range of stock. Quilted items she'd sewn, hand crafted jewellery, all the lovely things she made.

'I'm sure I'll see you at the fashion show. Perhaps we can even persuade you to strut your stuff on the runway,' she said, fishing to see if he'd be up for it. They wanted at least half a dozen men to take part in the show. So far, they only had two — Brodrick from the cafe bar and Lyle. Brodrick had agreed to walk with his girlfriend, Elspeth, down the runway, and Lyle said he'd accompany any of the ladies.

'I don't think I'm the strutting type,' Ean said, wriggling out of the offer.

Ailsa let him off the hook. 'That's fine. So, let me show you the new selection of watercolour paints.' She gestured to where they were displayed. 'See anything that catches your artistic eye?' Her smile lit up her beautiful features.

Ean's heart melted just looking at her. 'Yes.' He picked the colours he wanted and put them on the counter. 'I'll take one tube of each of these, and two extra tubes of the cerulean blue, Prussian blue, raw sienna and burnt sienna.'

Ailsa popped them in a bag for him and put it down on the counter while he paid for them. 'I wish I could paint like you. Your paintings hanging in the castle's reception are lovely.'

'Thank you,' he said, taking a deep breath, plucking up the courage to ask her to have dinner with him.

But the shop door opened and Rory strode in, looking fit and strong.

'Ailsa,' said Rory with a confident smile, 'Lyle mentioned about the fashion show at the castle. We're buying tickets. But I wanted to ask if you'd like to dance with me after the show, at the party. I haven't had a chance to talk to you as you've been away a lot, but I just saw you walking by the tea shop and...' he shrugged his broad shoulders under his denim shirt that he wore with blue jeans that were work worn, but flattered his lean–hipped build. His eyes were as pale blue as the well–washed denim and his hair was a fair match for the sand on the shore.

Ailsa sensed what else was coming. He wanted her to be his date. 'I'd be happy to dance with you, Rory. All the models will be enjoying the party and dancing with everyone.'

'Right,' Rory said, feeling curtailed. He glanced at Ean.

Sensing he was in the way, Ean smiled at Ailsa. 'Thanks for the watercolours.'

'I'll see you tonight at the castle,' she said.

Ean blinked.

'Skye and Holly have organised a meeting with Finlay to discuss the plans for the fashion show.'

'Oh, yes,' Ean said, feeling he was out of step with what she meant. He had remembered, but had worked himself up to ask her for a date, so all reasonable thoughts had gone to the wind. 'I'll see you later then.'

Smiling at her, Ean left the shop and stepped out into the sunlight, wishing that Rory hadn't interrupted. Or was that Rory's plan? Glancing back, he saw the good looking builder chatting her up, and his heart twisted.

Ean drove off back to the castle, hoping he hadn't missed his chance with Ailsa yet again.

As he drove along the harbour road towards the forest, his phone rang.

He pulled over and took the call from Geneen at the castle.

'You should give Ailsa your number, Ean,' she told him before adding, 'Ailsa phoned to say you've left your paints at her shop.'

Ean took a deep breath. 'Right, sorry, yes. I'll go and get them. Thanks, Geneen.'

'And give her your number,' Geneen said before they ended the call.

Ean drove back down and parked outside the craft shop.

'Forget something, Ean?' Rory said, smiling, as he left the shop and Ean walked in.

'I'm distracted with work. It's a busy morning,' Ean told him.

'Ailsa is a distraction in herself,' Rory quipped and then headed back to the tea shop.

Ailsa smiled and shook her head at Ean as she dangled the bag of paints in front of him.

He took the bag from her. 'I didn't leave them deliberately.'

She looked like she wasn't sure if she believed him.

'Can I give you my number?' he said. 'If you ever need to call me again, it'll save you phoning the castle.'

Ailsa nodded, and they exchanged numbers.

A customer came in before they could talk any more.

'I'll see you tonight at the castle,' Ailsa said to Ean and smiled as he left.

Rory walked into the traditional tea shop and approached Lyle who was adding cakes to one of his glass cabinet displays. Victoria sponges filled with cream and locally made strawberry jam were lit by spotlights, along with cupcakes swirled with chocolate buttercream, and lots of other delicious cakes and scones. Some of his cakes had a dash of whisky added to them, especially his rich fruit cakes, and the air often had a hint of his secret ingredient.

Lyle was late twenties, fairly tall and strong with light brown hair and hazel eyes. He wore a clean white shirt, black trousers and a chef's apron. He'd trained as a patisserie chef, and now owned the popular vintage style tea shop, having taken it over when his grandparents retired. So far, he'd made a success of it, and had asked Rory to help convert the upstairs floor of the two–storey shop to extend the premises. The work was to be done by the autumn, and was on schedule. The tea shop had remained open during the upstairs work, and Lyle planned a special event to launch the extension soon and promote his new autumn menu.

'Ailsa's looking extra beautiful these days. Is she seeing anyone?' Rory said to Lyle.

'You mean, does she have a boyfriend?'

'Aye.'

'No, she split with her boyfriend at the New Year. She'd been dating him for a long time, but according to the gossip, he left to take a job in London. Ailsa didn't want to leave the island. So...' Lyle shrugged.

'He left Ailsa?' Rory shook his head. 'She must've been upset.'

'No, they'd been drifting for a while, so it wasn't going to work out for them. But still...'

'Have you ever asked Ailsa to have dinner with you?'

'Out. Of. My. League.'

Rory laughed. 'What about Merrilees? She's a beauty too. You took a chance trying to date her.'

'When it comes to Merrilees, I have no sense.'

'What about Skye? She's become quite the loveliest I've ever seen her.'

Lyle shook his head. 'No, I like Skye. She's a bundle of fun, but too much of a livewire for me. I think she'd be a handful.'

'Holly's gorgeous, and more steady. I just don't know why you're not dating any of them.'

'That's not the question, or the answer. It's whether any of them would want to date me, and I think it's clear they're not interested,' said Lyle.

'How do you know?'

'I can tell by the way they don't look at me.'

Rory nodded, understanding. 'I know that look.'

'Why? Are you thinking of asking one of them out?'

'I'd like to have a date for the fashion show. I nearly asked Ailsa properly, but Ean was there.'

'The gossip is, Ean likes Ailsa.'

'I could tell by the snarly vibe when he saw me walking into the craft shop. And Ean's easy going, so he must really like that lassie.'

'Maybe set your sights elsewhere.'

'Or maybe not. Ean seems hesitant to ask Ailsa out on a date. Faint heart and all that won't win the day.'

'Don't go causing ructions,' Lyle told Rory.

'I won't. But if Ean takes the slow lane, I may just overtake him on the outside edge.'

Celia, forties and fabulous, editor of a fashion magazine in the city, sat at her desk, planning the features for the forthcoming issues. The magazine was a monthly publication, but the online edition had the ability to cut closer to deadlines when necessary if a feature merited it.

Celia had started up the magazine in Glasgow fairly recently, using her background working as a fashion editor for other magazines, to establish one of her own.

Immaculate from head to toe, with dark auburn hair smoothed sleek, makeup applied with professional precision emphasising her keen eyes, and can't miss it from a distance red lipstick, Celia drummed her manicured nails on the desk.

Her designer skirt suit was pink. And Celia never wore pastel. The exact colour was fuchsia petal cerise, and as fashion editor she was a stickler for exactness.

Celia's office was stylish, stark white and cedar. It didn't do pastel either.

Seona gave a token knock on Celia's door and then burst into the spacious office clasping what she believed to be a piece of editorial gold dust.

'Take a look at this.' Seona thrust a copy of a rival magazine at Celia, plopping it down in front of her and jabbed an urgent finger at Holly and Skye's feature.

Celia didn't bat an eyelid and merely glanced down at the two models wearing vintage evening dresses standing in front of a dress shop.

Seona, late twenties, dark blonde, and wearing high fashion, gave her a breathless with excitement short course of the feature culminating in, '...and their shop is on an island in Scotland.'

'Find out the name of the owners,' Celia said, snapping into urgent mode while still reading the feature, very taken with the beautiful dresses and the pretty shop. This could be just what they needed for the vintage fashion styling that was headlining a forthcoming issue.

'Holly and Skye own the shop,' Seona told her, showing her value as Celia's assistant, digging up nuggets worth polishing among the rubble of designer debris.

Celia tried not to frown as she said, 'The models? They own the shop? The two young women wearing the dresses?'

Seona nodded. 'It gets even better. They trained in fashion in the city, working in the fashion industry, designing and taking part in fashion shows. But their mother owned the vintage dress shop on the island, and gave it to them fairly recently to do with it whatever they wanted. They decided to sell vintage rather than high fashion, but included other clothes — skirts, tops, accessories, that sort of thing.'

Celia swept an uninterested hand in the air at the mention of the other clothes. 'These dresses are gorgeous.'

Seona pointed to the feature. 'It says here that their mother had a list of around a hundred contacts, built up over her years running the shop. They contacted her whenever they had vintage dresses available, often bulk buys, wardrobes full of treasure trove from upmarket house clearances, party dresses only worn once, that she then sold for a profit. That list was given to her daughters.'

'So they have numerous sources for top quality vintage.' Celia looked thoughtful. 'And they're young and have the model looks to carry this off. It's the perfect storm.'

'On an island,' Seona quipped.

Celia's lips formed a wry smile. 'What else is on this island? And where is it exactly?'

'It's twenty miles off the west coast of Scotland.' Seona's eyes glinted. 'And it has a fairytale castle with three handsome, young, eligible brothers running the castle and the estate. Turn over the page. One of them is pictured — Innis. Totally gorgeous.'

Celia's eyes widened. 'Totally. What agency is he with?'

Seona shook her head. 'No agency. Innis isn't a model. He helps his brothers run the castle. And he's a chocolatier with his own fancy cake shop on the island.'

'I'm liking this whole scenario. We'll hook Innis on board with us.'

'Innis is rich and successful. He may be difficult to persuade. He looks...not the easy going type. Brooding, hot, sexy.'

Ice cold eyes silenced any further description from Seona.

'I'm just saying,' Seona said and then beamed with enthusiasm. 'But Holly and Skye are holding a vintage fashion show at the castle...soon. The island has never had a fashion show before.'

'How soon?'

'Very.'

'Okay, send Cambeul to the island to get what we need.'

'No! Send me! Send me! I was the one who found this for you, Celia. I want to go to the island and stay in the fairytale castle.'

'Tell Cambeul not to drag his heels. Others will have their eye on this. Nail it for us. It's the first fashion show on the island. And the first time we've featured a fashion show on a Scottish island. That's the angle we'll take.'

Stomping out of the office, Seona closed the door on her plan. Sometimes it worked trying to wangle assignments to exotic places, sometimes it didn't. Not that the island was exotic, but it sounded wonderful. Fabulous fashion, a fairytale castle with handsome men, and one of them going to be a laird... She sighed heavily. It had been worth a try.

Celia looked at Holly and Skye's shop website address on the feature, typed at speed into her computer and found the phone number.

No hesitation. She called the shop.

CHAPTER THREE

Holly and Skye stood outside their shop looking up at the sign above the front window.

'So we agree,' said Holly. 'We'll take the new sign down and restore the shop to the way it was when mum had it last.'

Skye nodded. 'Yes, I loved the older sign. Let's not hesitate. We wanted publicity for the shop and now we've got it, so we should advertise the dresses to full advantage.'

'Murdo might help us again with the sign,' Holly said thoughtfully. 'We could ask him tonight when we're up at the castle.'

'We could, but...' Skye looked over at Lyle's tea shop and the builder's van parked outside it. 'Maybe we could ask the builder who's been converting the upper floor into an extension of the tea shop. When I was in buying an apple pie the other day, I heard Lyle telling someone that the work is nearly done. It's to be finished for the autumn. I don't know the builder, but it's that young man with the sandy blond hair. He's Lyle's cousin. Perhaps he could help us with the sign.'

'Yes, one of us should pop over and ask Lyle,' Holly agreed, looking straight at her sister.

'Okay, I'll do it,' said Skye.

While they were discussing this, Holly's phone rang.

Holly took the call from Celia. Very few words were exchanged on her part, as Celia told her precisely what she wanted. A vintage dress fashion feature for her magazine, expanding on the article in her rival's publication, and an interview to cover the fashion show at the castle.

Skye listened to the call on speaker, letting Holly handle it. Though it was really Celia calling the shots, but as the shots were what they'd aimed for, publicity for their vintage shop and fashion show, they agreed to do what Celia wanted.

Celia put the phone down. 'The ball's rolling,' she told Cambeul as he walked into her office, already armed to the teeth with the magazine featuring Holly, Skye and Innis.

'Seona is miffed,' he said.

Celia nodded.

'Just so you know.'

'I do. But I need your editorial and photographic skills to handle this assignment. Take your camera. I want lots of pics. Keep me updated. You know what to do to light a fire under this.'

He did.

Celia briefed him on the call she'd had with Holly, and the angle she wanted him to take for the assignment.

'Great, I'll catch the ferry over later today,' he said, and went to walk out of the office.

'Hold on. There's a new designer bag hanging over there.' She pointed to it on one of the rails in the far corner dripping with fashion pieces they'd used for recent photo–shoots.

He lifted it up and went to bring it over to her desk.

'It's for Seona. Give it to her on your way out.'

He smiled wryly. 'She'll faint when she gets this.'

'Remember, keep a lid on the island fashion feature. I don't want anyone else grabbing it from us,' Celia reminded him.

'I'll keep my suspicion antennae on alert,' he said, and walked away.

Skye walked into the tea shop. Lyle smiled as she approached the counter, thinking she'd come back for another apple pie or his special cupcakes.

'Could you ask your cousin, the builder, if he'd do a wee job for Holly and me?'

He blinked, taken aback, but happy to help her. 'Of course. Is it building work?'

'We want our shop sign taken down. We've decided to keep the original sign up. It's underneath the new one.'

'That shouldn't be too hard for him to do,' said Lyle. He hurried over to the stairs and called up to his cousin. 'Rory! Skye's here to ask you a favour.'

'It's not a favour,' she said. 'We'll pay him to do it.'

The sound of Rory's sturdy boots sounded on the stairs as he ran down, eager to help her.

'Pay me to do what?'

'Take our new shop sign down.' Skye explained the details.

'I'll grab my tool bag and tackle that right now for you,' Rory said, running back up the stairs.

'I don't want to interrupt his work for you at the tea shop,' Skye told Lyle.

'He's nearly finished,' Lyle assured her.

Skye smiled. 'Okay, that would be great. We're featured in a fashion magazine and another magazine saw the feature and now they want to interview us for their magazine too. It's all go. The editor from the magazine wants to emphasise the vintage dresses, so we want the original sign my mum had above the shop.'

Lyle gestured around his tea shop. 'The vintage styling really works for my business. It's a mix of vintage and modern, but customers love the atmosphere, and I bake lots of old–fashioned cakes and scones. So no wonder your vintage dresses are popular.' He admired the dress she was wearing. 'You're looking lovely today by the way.'

'Thank you, Lyle.'

Thunderous footsteps sounded on the stairs as Rory bounded down two at a time. 'Right, lead the way, Skye.'

She did, giving Lyle a cheery wave on her way out with the tall, good looking and very enthusiastic builder.

Skye led him over to the dress shop where Holly was busy sorting the mannequins in the window. She waved out to him.

He waved back. 'Morning, Holly.' Then he surveyed the shop sign and concluded, 'I'll sort the sign for you.'

'Bill us for the cost,' Skye reminded him.

'Nah, it's fine. This wee job is a skoosh. My ladders are in the van. I'll be back in a jiffy.'

He was. And the job was done faster than Skye or Holly anticipated as Rory's skill and strength removed the new sign to reveal the original one.

He put the new sign down on the pavement. 'Do you want to keep this one? I could drop it off at your house.'

'Would you? Our parents' house is that one up there on the hill near Ailsa's cottage. Leave it in the back garden. We'll store it in the shed. Our parents are away on the isle of Skye for a couple of weeks, visiting friends.'

'Will do.'

Holly came out and admired Rory's handiwork. 'That was fast.'

He grinned, pleased she was impressed.

'You have to take something for your work, Rory,' Skye told him.

Rory shook his head. 'Happy to help you young ladies out. But, I tell you what. I'll settle for a dance with you after the fashion show.'

They were surprised.

'You're going to our fashion show?' said Skye.

'Yes, Lyle suggested we get tickets. Everybody's going. I hear it'll be a fun night.'

'We'll save you a dance,' Skye promised him. As did Holly.

Smiling, Rory put their sign and his ladders in the back of his van and drove up the hill to drop the sign off at their parents' house.

Skye stood with her hands on her hips, admiring the vintage sign, while Holly finished dressing the mannequins in the window display. The front door was open to let in the warm, fresh sea air.

The shop's pink bicycle was often to be found parked outside, not just for decorative purposes. Skye and Holly used it to pop along the harbour road on errands that didn't merit taking their car. Skye loved the bike and enjoyed cycling along the coast on sunny days, feeling the sea breeze blow through her long hair.

Summertime bunting still decorated the shop's front window and added to the pretty display. It matched their pink floral tree.

'We should take photos of the shop front while the sun's out,' Holly called to her.

'Grab your camera. I'll finish the window display,' said Skye.

While Skye did this, Holly got her camera and stood outside to take the photographs.

'There, all done.' Skye stepped out of the window having sorted the display, and joined Holly outside.

'The shop looks great,' said Holly, taking several photos of it with the restored sign.

Skye peered at the images. 'It looks fantastic. We'll put these new pictures on the website.'

'Stand in front of the shop and I'll include you in a few,' said Holly.

Skye posed and smiled, and then she took photos of Holly outside the shop.

'I'll add these to the website,' Holly said, eager to get it updated.

Ailsa came hurrying along from her craft shop. 'I love the vintage dress shop sign.' Then she smiled.

'And I saw Rory flexing his muscles, trying to impress you.'

'It worked,' said Holly. 'We were impressed how fast he sorted it for us.'

'Lyle and Rory are going to the fashion show,' Skye told her. 'We've promised Rory a dance.'

'It's going to be a fun night,' said Ailsa.

'Have you promised to dance with Ean?' Skye said to Ailsa. 'We saw him going into your shop — twice.'

Ailsa explained what happened.

Holly and Skye exchanged a knowing look.

'Okay, so maybe Ean likes me a wee bit,' Ailsa admitted.

'More than a wee bit,' Holly told her. 'I think he's smitten.'

'Who's smitten?' a man's deep voice said from behind them.

They looked round and saw Innis walking out of his cake shop.

Ailsa blushed, feeling they'd been caught talking about his brother. 'Rory,' she fibbed.

Innis frowned. 'Smitten with you, Ailsa?'

'No, with Skye,' Ailsa said, uttering the first name she could think of.

Innis' reaction took them aback. 'Well, I'll let you ladies get on with your business.' He continued on his way.

Ailsa frowned at her friends. 'What was that look for? If I didn't know better, I'd say Innis was miffed.'

They agreed.

Ailsa sighed. 'Innis is a deep one. Whoever ends up dating the wolf is in for a deeply passionate time.'

'Passion and fashion,' Skye chirped. 'Not that I'd ever date the wolf. He's far too serious for me.'

Agreeing that none of them would end up involved with Innis, they got back to work in their shops.

Ean was back at the castle discussing the fashion show with Finlay and Murdo. They stood in the function room.

'I've an idea for the runway,' said Murdo. 'I can use some of the stage platform we've got in the storeroom. The pieces we use when businesses are here for presentations and things like that.'

'Would that be suitable as a runway for the models?' Finlay said to him.

'Oh yes. It's ideal, but I need to build another wee bit on to the end of it,' Murdo explained. 'I can do that, but I'll need to buy more wood.'

'Buy what you need to make it,' said Ean. 'I'll pay for it. But don't tell the ladies.'

'Aye, okay, nae fuss, Ean,' Murdo agreed.

'Ean and I have discussed this with Innis,' Finlay told Murdo. 'Ticket sales are doing well. It's going to be a packed night. We'll all do well from this, and it's great publicity for the castle and the community, so we don't want Skye and Holly out of pocket for sundries. But keep this to yourself.'

'I will,' Murdo assured them.

Geneen came into the function room. 'I've just taken a booking from a fashion magazine journalist. His name is Cambeul and his editor Celia is sending him to cover the fashion show. He'll be on the ferry tonight.'

'Great,' said Finlay. 'The more the merrier.'
Ean agreed.

Skye phoned Ailsa at the craft shop. 'Are you coming over for lunch? We're having lentil soup and salad.'

'I'm on my way. Do you want me to pick up a loaf?' Ailsa offered.

'No, it's fine. I bought bread this morning.'

Holly set up the lunch in the kitchen at the back of the shop while Skye finished stitching one of the dresses, repairing a seam, whizzing along it using her pink sewing machine. She secured the ends of the thread and then hung the dress on the repair rail alongside several others.

Ailsa came in and locked the shop door behind her. They closed their shops for lunch most days and often ate together, enjoying having a chat, especially when they had plans to make for the fashion show.

They sat at the kitchen table, eating their soup and a crisp green salad with slices of fresh bread. A pot of tea sat on the table, and they helped themselves to everything while they discussed their plans.

'We're putting all the dresses we have on to the rails in the shop,' Holly explained, 'and moving the other items, like the jackets and trousers, through to the storeroom. We'll still sell those, but they don't sell fast and they're taking up too much room in the shop.'

'Was that a new delivery of dresses I saw on the rail beside the counter?' said Ailsa.

'Yes, they're beautiful quality. All the same size, so we think they must've come from a house clearance. Some of them are designer pieces,' Holly added.

'The dresses are barely worn,' said Skye. 'Probably worn once for a special party and then hung in the wardrobe. There are chiffon and velvet numbers, so whoever bought them wore them for different seasons. One of the dresses is dripping with sparkling beads and was maybe worn to a Christmas party. It's got that look to it.'

'I love vintage beadwork, especially for cocktail party dresses,' Ailsa told them.

'We're sorting the dresses after lunch,' said Holly. 'And putting aside what we'll be including in the fashion show.'

'Do you need a hand?' Ailsa offered. 'I can keep an eye on my shop from the window and run along if I have a customer. I've already packed my online orders for the day and dropped them off at the post office.'

'That would be great,' Holly told her. 'And it'll let us discuss what would be suitable for the show.'

They finished lunch, drank down their tea and then started rearranging the dresses and other vintage items.

Ailsa held up a drop waist shimmering cocktail dress. 'What colour would you say this is? Champagne?'

'Pink champagne,' Skye suggested. 'We should definitely include it in the show.'

'Try it on,' Holly encouraged Ailsa. 'See if it fits you.'

Ailsa stepped into the small changing room and pulled the curtain. 'Keep an eye on my shop for me.'

They did.

A few minutes later, Ailsa stepped out wearing the dress. She waggled, causing the beads to swish back and forth. 'I could get my wiggle on with this dress,' she joked.

They giggled.

'You should wear it for the show. It really suits you,' Holly told her.

Skye agreed. 'We're having a cocktail party dress selection. That one is a winner.'

Holly lifted a gold sequin sheath dress from a rail. 'I'm planning to wear this one.' She held it up in front of her. The gold lit up her face. 'All that glitters...' She smiled, happy with her selection. She showed them the shoes she intended wearing with it — gold, thirties style with medium height heels and ankle straps.

Skye unhooked the dress she was wearing for the cocktail range — a little gold lamé number, and set aside a pair of rounded toe gold shoes with mid heels.

'From flapper to fabulous,' said Skye, taking a note for the commentary they planned to accompany the dresses.

'We've asked Nettie and Morven to do the commentary,' Holly explained. 'They'll sit on the stage, at the side, and give a running commentary of the dresses as the models walk down the runway.'

Morven owned the knitting shop, and had recently invited her niece, Elspeth to join her in running the shop and the knitting bee. Elspeth was now dating Brodrick from the cafe bar, and Morven was back from an extended holiday on the mainland with her new boyfriend, Donall. Morven and Donall were in their fifties and discovered that they'd both liked each other for a while, but neither had told the other until recently.

Nettie, forties, was another member of the knitting bee and they felt she was a confident speaker and wouldn't faff things up.

'And we've invited a few friends that own vintage dress shops in Glasgow and Edinburgh,' Skye added. 'Delphine owns the fairytale tea dress shop in Edinburgh.'

'Oh, I know Delphine,' said Ailsa. 'I hope she comes to the fashion show.'

'Delphine phoned me to confirm she'll be there,' Skye told her. 'Others I've asked that are coming are Esmie, owner of the vintage tea dress shop on the west coast down from Glasgow. And Joyce and Bee. I love their vintage fashion shop in Glasgow and the way they repair and upscale vintage dresses.'

'I've met them on the fashion circuits too,' Ailsa told them. 'They're lovely.'

'We're all into having vintage dress bargains,' said Holly. 'Enabling customers to look great for less — champagne chic for lemonade money.'

Skye nodded firmly. 'Exactly. So they're all coming along to support us at the fashion show.'

'Will your parents be back from their holiday on the Isle of Skye in time to see the fashion show?' said Ailsa.

Holly shook her head. 'No, the dates clash with their friends' anniversary party on the island. That's part of the reason they went to the island, to enjoy all the celebrations with their friends. They offered to cut their holiday short to come back for our show, but we've told them it's fine. We've promised to take lots of photos and we're having a video of the whole show so they won't miss out seeing it.'

'Besides, we've invited Delphine, Esmie, Joyce and Bee to stay at our house after the show,' Skye told Ailsa. 'With our parents away and two spare rooms, we're having a fun sleepover.'

Ailsa laughed, picturing the giggling and chaos.

'You're welcome to join us,' said Skye. 'You know us, we'll be having so much fun we'll be lucky to get to our beds before the dawn.'

'I know,' Ailsa agreed. 'I'll think about it.'

'I suppose it'll depend on whether you're walking hand in hand in the moonlight with a handsome young man,' Holly teased her.

'I don't think so!' Ailsa protested lightly.

Skye smiled at Ailsa. 'We'll see.'

Rosabel and Primrose waved in the window.

Skye opened the door and let them in.

'We're on our lunch break,' Rosabel explained. 'But we wondered if we should select our dresses for the show. You said to drop by, so...'

'Yes, come on in. We're nailing the cocktail dress section,' said Skye.

'There are plenty of lovely cocktail length dresses on those two rails over there,' Holly said, pointing to the rails packed with dresses.

Holly and Skye wanted to include more mature models as well as younger ones in the show, and had invited Rosabel and Primrose to participate.

Primrose gravitated to her favourite colour — pale yellow, and held up a pretty, drop-waist dress. 'Can I try this one on?'

'Yes, try whatever you want,' Holly told them.

Between them, the women selected their cocktail dresses, with Rosabel opting for a pastel pink chiffon party dress that flattered her figure and silvery curls.

Ailsa had to pop along to her shop a couple of times, but spent the remainder of the afternoon helping out at the vintage dress shop, after Rosabel and Primrose headed back to Innis' cake shop.

An amber glow shone across the sea as the day came to a close, making the sea look like liquid bronze.

'We'll get something to eat at the castle,' Skye suggested as they continued to work in the dress shop until it was time to drive up to the castle for their meeting with Finlay, Ean and Murdo.

'Will Innis be there too?' Ailsa said to them.

Skye sighed and nodded.

'Do you think he'll have something snippy to say about being in the magazine?' said Ailsa.

'Nooo,' Skye lied, and then giggled.

They all laughed.

'It should be an interesting night.' Holly hung up a full-length dark blue satin dress along with a dazzling red sequin design that Ailsa had said she'd wear.

'We should dress up for the meeting,' Skye said with a sudden burst of enthusiasm. 'No jeans or pretty casuals. Let's dress to impress.'

Holly nodded. 'Without being ridiculously over the top.'

Ailsa was up for this. 'Just enough sparkle to make a fashionable entrance.'

Riffling through the rails, they each picked what they'd wear, and then started getting ready to head to the castle.

CHAPTER FOUR

'Are you here on holiday?' the taxi driver said to Cambeul as he drove him along the forest road to the castle. The evening was still early, and the glow of an amber sun cast a golden glow across the sea in the distance as they headed away from the harbour.

Fresh off the ferry, and after a hectic day organising everything so he could be there that night, Cambeul was in no mood for chit–chat.

'No, work.'

'Well, it's a fine castle to work from. I'm sure you'll enjoy your stay. The meals are delicious, the rooms are sumptuous with great views of the island, and the staff and owners are a delight to know,' the driver told him. In his forties, the man was a cheery chatty type.

'I'm sure I will.' Cambeul sat in the back seat, uninterested in the scenery. Lots of trees and more trees swept by as they drove along a narrow road lit by the car headlights. He still felt the motion of the ferry. Boats weren't his thing. He even imagined he could hear the noise of the ferry churning through the water, like someone with a snotty nose snoring faintly in the back of his mind. He needed a good night's sleep, on dry land.

'If you have a keek out the window, you'll see the castle turrets through the trees,' the driver encouraged him.

Cambeul leaned wearily over to the window and peered out. And blinked. He'd anticipated a castle, but sort of expected it to be like a big, posh, castellated mansion, or a crumbling monstrosity in need of repair and suffering from damp. But the castle that he glimpsed was nothing like that. He should've checked their website prior to getting on the ferry, but his whirlwind day hadn't allocated time for common sense.

The journalist in him sparked into overdrive, and the enthusiasm he kept on standby, in case of exclusive story emergencies, switched on.

'Tell me about the castle. I'm meeting Finlay and Ean. They're brothers.'

'Fine young men they are. And you'll meet the third brother too, Innis. He's the talk of the island the noo. Got himself into a bit of a romantic pickle and ended up having his photies in a fancy fashion magazine. All the lassies are buying copies from the grocers to have a gander at him.'

Cambeul scrambled to get his notepad and pen from his laptop bag. 'A romantic pickle?' he prompted the taxi driver. Writing down on the pad:

Innis — romantic pickle.

'Yes, Skye and Holly were taking pictures of themselves outside their vintage dress shop in the springtime. They were being included in a fashion feature in a city magazine. Anyway, Skye encouraged Innis to get his photie taken with them too, and here's the pickle — Innis is a good man, but he's not what you would call...awfy accommodating, so the rumour is that he must really like one of the lassies to have gone along with this. And folk reckon he's got a secret fancy for Skye.'

Cambeul scribbled in his notepad:
Innis secretly fancies Skye.

'Do you know Skye and Holly?' said Cambeul.

'Not really, just to see and nod to. For years, they lived on the mainland, training and working in fashion. But I knew their mother. She used to own the vintage dress shop. My wife, Nettie, bought lovely frocks from there. Now she buys from Skye and Holly. Nettie's even doing the running commentary at their fashion show. It's being held at the castle next week. Will you be staying long enough to go to it?'

Nettie — commentating fashion show.

'I will. So, eh, is your wife, Nettie, experienced in commentary work?'

'Och, no. She's just a chatterbox, a bit like myself, so they've asked her because she'll not run out of gabble. Morven is helping as well with the commentary. They're working it between them.'

'Morven?'

'She owns the local knitting shop. She runs it now with her niece, Elspeth, who moved here from Glasgow fairly recently. Elspeth loves working in the knitting shop with her Aunt Morven. And she's fallen in love with Brodrick the owner of the cafe bar.'

Aunt Morven and Nettie — fashion show commentary.

Elspeth — works with her Aunt Morven, owner of knitting shop. Elspeth loves Brodrick — cafe bar owner.

'Romance has flourished recently on the island. It goes through cycles like that. No romance, then bam, bam, bam. One after the other. So far this summer we've had Elspeth and Brodrick, and Finlay and Merrilees.'

'Merrilees?'

'She's a newspaper journalist from Glasgow.'

Cambeul jolted at the mention of a newspaper journalist.

The driver checked the time. 'I'm scheduled to pick Merrilees up at the harbour tonight off the last ferry. She's been working all day at the newspaper office. I'll pick her up and drive her to the castle. She doesn't bother taking her car over to the city these days. She just jumps on the ferry and uses taxis. Finlay often drops her off in the morning when it's her day working at the paper. But because he's usually busy with the party nights at the castle, I pick her up from the ferry.'

Merrilees — newspaper journalist, Glasgow. Ferry from island.

'But Merrilees and Finlay are the big romance of the moment. She's a lovely lassie. He'll be the laird one day.'

Merrilees, big romance with Finlay the future laird.

'Anyway, the magazine came out today and it has a few juicy pictures of Innis in it along with Skye and Holly's story. Now I've heard that another fancy magazine wants to do a story about them and their vintage fashions. And Nettie says the rumour about Innis having a secret notion of Skye will be the talk of the knitting bee tomorrow night.'

'So, it's a secret?' Cambeul's journalistic tone came to the fore.

'Aye, and maybe the rumours are wrong, so whatever you're scribbling down, put in brackets — long shot.'

Cambeul put the notepad aside and sighed. 'My editor, Celia, owns the fancy magazine that's covering the fashion show and the vintage dress shop feature. She's sent me to write the editorial and take photographs. The current story, the one with pictures of Innis, is in Celia's rival magazine. So she wants our magazine to write an exclusive vintage fashion feature.'

'Will you be putting in any raunchy photos of Innis?'

'Doubtful. We're just interested in the fashion. Celia phoned Skye and Holly and they're happy to let us cover their show. Finlay knows too. I'm not working undercover. Is there anyone you think I should talk to or interview?'

'Talk to Merrilees. She wrote about the businesses on the island recently for the newspaper. One of those supplements, like a magazine. She did a great job. Everyone was happy with what she wrote and the photos she took of us.'

Talk to Merrilees.

'And you should pop along to the knitting bee tomorrow night. Seven o'clock at the knitting shop. All the ladies, including my Nettie, will be there. You'll find out all the news, and the gossip, and be spoiled rotten with tea and cake.'

Cambeul smiled. 'I'll do that.' And then he sighed heavily. 'I didn't bring my yoga mat with me. Not enough room in my luggage. But I assume the castle has a gym for guests.'

'Nooo. And if you ask, you'll just get pointed towards the castle's estate gardens, the forest, nature's gym. But you look fit and strong to me. A trek through the forest is a great workout. Ean goes hill running. Go for a run with him. Have a jaunt around thistle loch, and a wee dip in the waterfall.'

'It all sounds very...outdoor adventurous.'

'Not your thing?'

'I don't know. I tend to go to the gym.'

'Maybe try and get some fresh air in your lungs while you're here. And remember, there's lively dancing most nights at the castle. The parties are a workout in themselves.'

'I suppose I could be persuaded to join in with the jigging.'

'The ceilidh nights are lively. You can hire a kilt from the castle. But go commando underneath it. It's great to get some air about your danglers.'

Cambeul laughed. And then his phone rang.

'It's my editor. I need to talk to Celia in private.'

The driver pulled the taxi over and parked.

Cambeul stepped out on to the grassy verge to take the call.

'Watch your step,' the driver called out to him. 'Don't wander off. You won't see the rough in the dark.'

Cambeul brushed aside this advice and wandered away from the taxi while talking to Celia. Though she did most of the talking while he listened.

Then she said, 'Hang on, there's a call from New York. I have to take this. I'll put you on hold.'

Click.

Cambeul huffed and continued to wander and then gazed up at the night sky, fascinated to see hundreds of stars. The evening was so clear. A vast sky arching overhead twinkling with—

'Argh!' Cambeul took a tumble in the rough, rolled down a shallow hill and then scrambled his way back up. His designer cargo trousers, shirt and expensive casual jacket, all in light cream and beige tones, were covered in grass, heather and dirt.

Stomping back to the taxi, highlighted by the headlight beams, he muttered to himself and brushed the debris from his nice clothes.

He got into the back seat, still brushing his trousers.

'Here, wipe the dirt off your trews with this.' The driver handed him over a small blanket from the passenger seat.

Cambeul accepted it, grateful to have something to clean his trousers.

The driver turned the overhead light on so Cambeul could see what he was doing.

That's when Cambeul noticed...

'This blanket is covered in cat hair.' He looked aghast.

'Aye, it's the cat's blankie.'

'Bleurgh!' Cambeul dropped it as if it was infested. 'What are you doing with a cat's blanket on the passenger seat?'

The driver scooped up the cute black and white cat on the seat beside him and held it up. 'I'm kitten sitting.'

Cambeul blinked, having a cat almost shoved in his face.

'He doesn't like being left on his own in the house. Nettie's out with her friends for a chinwag, so when I'm doing my taxi work, I take Fluffy with me.'

The cat was between a kitten and a young cat, a bundle of sleepy fluff, paws dangling, yawning, then falling asleep again.

'Fluffy's at that age where everything's an adventure. He's been playing in the garden all day and tuckered himself out.'

The snoring. Cambeul realised...

The driver reached over, grabbed the blanket and set it down on the passenger seat again along with the cat.

Cambeul saw the driver's ID in the light. 'Shuggie.'

'Aye, that's me. I didn't catch your name.'

'Cambeul. Here's my card. Contact me if you think of anyone else I should interview.'

Shuggie accepted the card and handed Cambeul one in return. 'Here's mine. Phone if you need a lift when you're on the island.'

And then he clicked the light off and drove on towards the entrance gates of the castle.

The ornate gates were open wide, overarched by the trees, creating an entrance that led into the castle gardens, akin to a park with lawns and flower beds.

Climbing roses and other florals clambered up parts of the castle's dark stone structure.

Perhaps it was the night time that made Cambeul so in awe he found himself staring, unblinking, at the castle in a setting that was straight out of a fairytale.

'The warrior trees look impressive at night,' said Shuggie.

'Warrior trees?'

'The tall, dark pines, around the outer edges of the castle gardens. The silhouettes look like ancient warriors guarding the castle from invaders.'

Cambeul looked again and saw exactly that. 'Stop the car. I want to take pics of this scene.'

Shuggie pulled over and Cambeul grabbed his camera and clicked several pictures of the castle lit up, the windows and wide open doorway aglow with lights, bordered by the warrior trees against the night sky filled with stars.

Cambeul got back in the car, feeling exhilarated. Celia would love these pics. Very dramatic. They could overlay them with fashion images for the online edition of the magazine where they extended the features with extra pics.

'...and make sure you do that!' Celia's voice sounded from Cambeul's phone. He'd been so busy taking the photos he hadn't realised. The phone was sitting on the back seat.

Cambeul grabbed the phone. 'I'm on it,' he bluffed as she ended the call abruptly having to take another call from New York.

'I thought I heard somebody yabbering from your phone. Celia sounds...' Shuggie searched for a nice comment. 'The efficient and go–getter type.'

Cambeul nodded, no elaboration.

Shuggie drove on towards the front of the castle.

'You should go for a dip in the sea while you're here,' said Shuggie. 'That'll keep you fit.'

'Is the sea temperate this time of year?'

'The sea around the island is rarely deceitful. If the sea looks cold, it'll be freezing. If it looks warm, it's probably warm enough.'

'I enjoy swimming, though it's been years since I've been in the sea. I do lengths of the pool at the gym facility.'

'Well, maybe it's time to go for a dip doon the shore in the watter,' said Shuggie, parking the car right outside the castle.

The castle rose from the night in all its splendour.

Cambeul gazed out the window, admiring the turrets spiralling high into the night sky. The castle looked majestic.

A tall, handsome, blond–haired figure was backlit by the glow from the castle's reception.

'That's Finlay waiting to greet you,' said Shuggie as Cambeul paid his fare and added a tip.

Finlay stood at the entrance wearing his black and dark grey tartan kilt, white shirt and black waistcoat, looking the epitome of what he was supposed to be.

First impressions counted, Cambeul reminded himself. He always tried to make a great first impression. A last frantic brush of his trousers to remove any excess cat hair, and he was ready to meet the prospective laird. Finlay had already made a good impression by standing in the doorway all lit up.

'I'll get your luggage,' said Shuggie, taking the bags from the boot.

A member of the castle staff picked the bags up and carried them inside to reception. Other staff were seen milling around in the reception, ready to attend to the new arrival.

Ean headed through them to join Finlay, wearing his black and dark grey tartan kilt, white shirt and waistcoat. Ean wore cream woollen knee–length socks with his brogues, and the lean muscles in his legs from all the hill running were evident as he strode towards the entrance.

Cambeul stepped out and gazed up at the magnificent castle, momentarily in awe of where he was.

Shuggie got back in the taxi, and with a cheery wave shouted to Cambeul. 'Remember to wear a kilt to the dancing, Cambeul. And give your swingers an airing.'

Shuggie's comment sounded loud and clear in the still night air, causing everyone from Cambeul to Finlay and Ean and the staff, to pause, suck up any remarks or laughter, and pretend it was never said.

Cambeul smiled tightly as Finlay stepped forward and extended his hand.

'Lovely to meet you, Cambeul,' Finlay said, and gestured towards the entrance. 'We're delighted to have you as our guest at the castle.'

'Pleased to meet you, Finlay,' said Cambeul, following him into reception.

'This is my brother, Ean.'

They shook hands.

'We're having a meeting with Holly and Skye in the function room to discuss the fashion show. You're welcome to join us,' Ean offered.

'Eh, yes, that would be great,' said Cambeul, wishing he could've gone to his room, but willing to take the opportunity to meet the vintage dress shop owners.

'Staff will take your luggage up to your room,' Finlay told Cambeul, leading him into the function room lit with chandeliers and that had an expensive ballroom quality to it with windows overlooking the castle's back patio and gardens beyond.

Cambeul admired the stylish decor. He appreciated tasteful design. The plush tartan carpeting was in shades of dark grey and black. The walls were white and beige with oak beams, and in reception the table lamps created a welcoming glow and highlighted the exquisite paintings hanging up depicting the castle and estate, countryside and seascapes in both oils and watercolours. Celia would've approved of the colour scheme.

Guests were seated at tables around the edges of the dance floor, having dinner or drinks. Couples were already taking to the floor, and everyone was well–dressed for the occasion. Cambeul's experienced eye noted a couple of designer dresses. Money dresses, and other ready–to–wear ensembles of fair merit. Vintage was present and accounted for too, with several ladies wearing classic thirties to fifties dresses. Acquired from Holly and Skye's vintage dress shop?

Something to enquire about when he met them to discuss their shop.

A live band played on the small stage where Cambeul rightly assumed the fashion models would emerge from. One step down and they would be able to walk across the dance floor, unless a runway was planned for the show. A runway was his preference, but as this was the first fashion show on the island he doubted they had one of those tucked away in storage. If that was the case, he'd insist on a front row seat to take notes at the show. He needed to see the dresses in full and not have to guess about the hemlines and other aspects. Writing fashion features was his forte, and he'd dated a few models in his time. Lovely ladies, but he'd yet to find a lasting love in the world of high fashion. Maybe he'd meet her in vintage.

A table in the far corner had been allocated as Finlay's private table where he entertained guests. Skye, Holly and Ailsa were seated there, awaiting Finlay and Ean rejoining them.

Even at this distance, Cambeul's astute eye for fashion was sure they were wearing vintage. A nice touch, he thought, for their vintage fashion show meeting in this classic setting.

'This is like a...fairytale castle,' Cambeul remarked to Finlay and Ean, gazing around him, summing up the whole impression.

'That's what people often call it,' said Finlay. 'A fairytale castle.'

CHAPTER FIVE

Shuggie picked up Merrilees at the harbour as she arrived off the last ferry of the night.

He opened the door for her, and she sat in the back with her laptop and another large shoulder bag stuffed with her day's work from the newspaper office.

She reached over and gave Fluffy a gentle pat and then relaxed back. 'Fluffy looks like I feel.'

'Weary from your work at the newspaper?'

'A hectic day,' she said. Merrilees was in her late twenties with shoulder–length blonde hair, a lovely pale complexion and grey eyes. She wore a white blouse, black jacket and black trousers that suited her slim figure.

Shuggie drove off, heading along the main street at the harbour and then up into the countryside towards the forest road leading to the castle. The change in scenery from seascape to a deep forest made the journey an enchanting experience. One minute there was the sea sparkling in the moonlight, and the next, thick trees overarching a road that looked like it was leading into a fairytale forest.

Although the drive was short, the transition seemed to make her relax, as if she shrugged off the workload of a day in the city, and like the pages of a storybook, she'd turned to emerge in a new chapter where her real life existed, albeit in a fairytale setting.

'We've got a newcomer to the island,' Shuggie told her. 'He arrived tonight from Glasgow and booked into the castle. I drove him there. He's staying for a week to cover the fashion show. His name is Cambeul and he's a magazine journalist.'

Merrilees reacted to the mention of *journalist*. 'Friend or foe?'

'Friend, I'd say, but then I'm the trusting sort.'

'I'll take him as that then, unless he gives me reason to think otherwise.' She'd heard about the fiasco with Innis being in the fashion magazine with Skye and Holly's feature. Finlay had phoned to tell her at the newspaper.

'He's a city wise, media type, like yourself. No offence, Merrilees.'

'None taken, Shuggie. I'll keep that in mind.'

'He wants to interview folk about the fashion show and the vintage dress shop. He's writing the feature for his editor. I hope it's okay, but I recommended he talk to you. I thought you'd know how to handle him.'

'That's fine. I'm curious to meet him and find out what his angle is for the feature.'

Shuggie told her the name of the magazine. 'It's in your turf, Glasgow.'

'I'm familiar with that publication. It's a fairly new magazine.'

'He said his editor's name is Celia.'

'Yes, that's right,' Merrilees recalled.

The taxi pulled up outside the castle, and there was Finlay standing waiting to greet her.

'Thanks for the tip–off, Shuggie.' She paid him and added a generous bonus for his trouble.

'The wanderer returns.' Finlay opened his arms wide to welcome her.

She stepped into his warm embrace, feeling his strong arms around her, lifting her off her feet, bags and all.

'One day I'll stop the wandering,' she promised, hoping it would be soon. She was working hard on finishing her romance novel, as requested by a publisher interested in her story.

'We're having a meeting about the fashion show.' Finlay gestured into the function room where she saw Holly, Skye and Ailsa sitting, along with Ean.

'Do I need to attend?' said Merrilees.

'No,' Finlay told her.

'Should I?'

'Yes.'

'Okay, I'll dump my things in my room and be right down.' She hurried up the private staircase to her room on the first floor near Finlay's suite further along the hallway.

Shrugging off her jacket along with her tiredness, the journalist in her kicked into action and she quickly checked information about Celia's magazine on her laptop.

Skim reading the website, she ingested what she needed to know and brushed aside the chicken feed. Armed with enough knowledge about the magazine, Celia and Cambeul, whose unsmiling picture she saw on the website, she brushed her hair, touched up her makeup and headed down into the fray.

'Would you care to join us for dinner? Or did you eat on the ferry?' Finlay said to Cambeul.

'I'm not great with boats, sailing, so all I had was a latte,' Cambeul confessed.

Finlay handed him a menu. 'You'll be hungry then.'

Cambeul wasn't particularly peckish until he read the menu, tempted by more dishes than he could ever chomp his way through. By the time he'd eaten everything that appealed to his taste buds, chef would've come up with another speciality to grab his appetite's attention.

Cambeul and Merrilees were the last of the group to order. The others' main dishes were being served.

'Don't wait for me,' Merrilees said to them with a smile, having been introduced to Cambeul by Finlay.

They started to tuck in.

'I haven't had anything since a bowl of soup for lunch,' said Skye. Her choice of vintage dress emphasised her preference for flirty florals, and she'd worn her hair down but pinned up at the sides with butterfly clips. 'None of us have,' she added to include Holly and Ailsa.

Holly wore vintage velvet like it was made for her. Midnight blue, figure skimming with a tasteful split. Her chestnut hair was swept up in a sophisticated chignon and her makeup was forties fabulous.

Skye and Holly had both ordered the speciality pasta with its rich tomato sauce, garnished with fresh lemon and a sprinkling of cheese.

Cambeul opted for the baked salmon and fresh vegetables. He surreptitiously took in the styling of the dresses worn by Skye and Holly, and although admitting that they were model–like beautiful, it was

Ailsa's classic beauty that captured his special attention. She. Was. Gorgeous. Totally his type. He'd been badly burned by the Ailsas of this world, but was willing to endure another few scorch marks if she was interested in him. He could see why Innis would have a secret fancy for Skye, if the rumour was true.

'Is Innis joining us?' Cambeul said, fanning the flames of intrigue. 'I was hoping to meet him.'

'He's busy in the castle kitchen making chocolates,' Finlay told him. 'The interest in him has caused customers to pop into his cake shop, and they've cleared him out of almost every box of chocolates he has. So, our head chef, Ailsa's uncle by the way, is helping Innis with his chocolatier work.'

'That's right, Innis is a chocolatier. How fascinating,' said Cambeul. 'Perhaps after dinner I could see him at work in the kitchen?'

'I'll ask him,' said Finlay. 'But he's very busy this evening.'

This didn't put Cambeul off his objective. 'I do enjoy seeing artisans like Innis at work. Do you or Ean specialise in any additional work of a creative nature, or do you just run the castle?'

'The castle takes up our time,' Finlay told him.

Ailsa jumped in with a comment. 'Ean is a wonderful artist. His paintings are hanging in reception. I love his watercolours.'

Did she love Ean? This was Cambeul's first reaction, and now he noticed how Ean looked at Ailsa. The attraction was there from Ean, but he couldn't tell if Ailsa just liked Ean without any further depths of interest. But he'd find out. He always did.

Ean smiled, but made no fuss, something that told Cambeul he had a real talent for art. Some of the best creative types didn't fanfare their skills. Yes, he thought, he'd check out the paintings later. Piece by piece, he'd find the nuggets of gold worth polishing and using to add to the feature to make it shine. Love, lust, desire and heartbreak never went out of style, and often complemented his fashion editorials with a bit of gossipy drama. Even if it didn't, he was the nosey sort par excellence.

Ailsa certainly intrigued him. He dug around until he brought the conversation around to her modelling work.

'What agency are you with?' Cambeul said to Ailsa, prepared to come up empty as he had done regarding Innis.

Ailsa told him the name of the agency.

Cambeul was duly impressed. A strong, mid range agency, but with her looks, Ailsa could reach the top. 'Have you ever considered taking your modelling work further, focussing solely on that part of your career rather than running your craft shop?'

'No,' she replied. 'My modelling work supplements my craft business that I'm building up. If I took my modelling career further, I'd have to travel the globe, or at least make regular trips to London, where I've been offered work already. But I don't want to leave the island, at least, not for longer than a week or two, and even then, I'm always happy to come home.'

'With your looks, you could go right to the top,' Cambeul told her.

Ailsa blushed. She looked gorgeous in the fifties tartan dress she was wearing.

'Is your dress genuine vintage?' Cambeul said to Ailsa. 'I'm interested to know the market for pre–loved tartan designs.'

'It is,' Ailsa confirmed. 'Skye and Holly's shop has a full rail of vintage tartan dresses ranging from forties and fifties flared dresses to pencil styles.'

Skye jumped in give him further details. 'We've acquired numerous plaid and tartan dresses from our contacts. When customers think of vintage, tartan isn't usually their first image. A classic tea dress or polka dot fit and flare number is what most of them think of. So we're actively seeking more pre–loved tartan dresses and our sources are confident they can supply us with them.'

'Scottish vintage is going to be part of our fashion show,' Holly told Cambeul. 'Tartan and plaid dresses are becoming very popular with our customers.'

'This is something that Celia wants me to emphasise in the feature,' said Cambeul.

'All to the good then,' Finlay said, cutting in with a confidence that reminded Cambeul that he was a guest.

'Anyone for sticky toffee pudding?' one of the waiting staff said chirpily. 'It's chef's special pud this evening.

'I'll skip dessert,' said Cambeul.

He was the only one.

'Shuggie mentioned that you're a hill runner,' Cambeul said to Ean.

'I am. Are you into this yourself?'

'No, I train at the gym, but I may go for a run around the castle grounds to keep fit while I'm here.' Cambeul waited for an invitation to join Ean, but found none.

'The sea is still mild if you're into swimming,' Ean told him.

'I'll probably go for a swim in the morning,' said Cambeul.

After finishing their dinner, Ean suggested they take a look backstage where Murdo was waiting to talk to them about his plans for the runway.

'Hello, folks,' Murdo said cheerily, and with enthusiasm for his ideas backed with sketches of what he had in mind.

'The castle has a runway that is used for business presentations,' Murdo explained, showing them rough sketches of it. 'There's a wee bitty missing that I'm hammering together, but this should surely give you a nice walkway to show your models wearing the dresses.'

Holly and Skye's eyes widened.

'This is even better than we imagined,' Holly told Murdo.

Ailsa nodded. It was on a par with some of the runways she'd been on recently during her excursions to the mainland to participate in fashion and photographic assignments.

Ean tried to keep his heart in check, but Ailsa looked particularly beautiful this evening. Her dress emphasised her slender curves, and her dark hair shone like watered silk. Every time her azure eyes glanced at him, he felt a jolt of excitement charge through him. Hopefully she didn't notice. The timing was inappropriate, but when it came to falling for Ailsa, he couldn't help it.

Cambeul opened a folder of notes stacked with editorial pieces from previous issues of the magazine, along with a mockup of the feature he was planning, from his laptop bag. He laid it down on a table backstage.

'Is that the magazine's pagination sheets for the forthcoming issue, the one featuring the fashion show and vintage dress shop?' Merrilees said to Cambeul.

Taken aback by her knowledge and keen observation, Cambeul's defence system was overridden, and he openly handed her a copy.

Before he could change his mind and swipe it back from her eyes that scanned it like a barcode, she assessed that a considerable section of the magazine had been allocated to the feature.

'Celia plans to headline the issue with the fashion show feature, highlighting the vintage dresses, and with a cherry on top extra about Scottish vintage dresses. The slant we're taking is — it's the first fashion on the island, the first time our magazine has featured a fashion show on an island, and a spotlight on Scottish vintage dresses. Something fresh for our readers.'

'Excellent,' said Merrilees. 'That's at least two double page spreads,' she added, eyeing the pagination sheets. 'Is that real allocation, or wishful thinking?'

'Real,' Cambeul told Merrilees. 'We're headlining strong with the vintage dress fashion. Celia has a nose for what's popular, and she's sussed out that this is what we need for the forthcoming issue. The online version will expand on whatever we put in the hard copy of the magazine, so that's why I'm widening the scope to include edits with pics of various scope and size. We're talking word counts of five hundred, like your newspaper ad–feats I'm sure, with plenty of visuals, especially as it's fashion. Readers love to see the dresses.'

Merrilees and Cambeul talked shop for a couple of minutes while the others listened.

Cambeul concluded. 'The leading editorial, Holly and Skye's background and current story, will be expanded on and everything else will be smaller, but very few sound bites. Nibbles are not for us. Our readers like a little bit more meat on the bones of their features, and that's what I'm here for, to glean as much info as I can to write it.'

Skye and Holly looked at Merrilees, trusting her to know what was right for them. The feature she'd written about them for the newspaper supplement recently had worked well, and her experience was of value in this instance to deal with Cambeul and his magazine.

Merrilees gave them an assuring nod, and then said, 'I noticed you've got a new shop sign up.'

'Yes,' said Holly, and explained what they'd done.

'Restoring the original shop sign is a great idea,' said Merrilees. 'I saw it when I got off the ferry tonight.'

'We've added it to our website and we think it looks better,' Holly told her.

'Would it be okay if I popped down to have a look around your shop tomorrow?' Cambeul said to Holly and Skye.

They agreed he should pop in during the afternoon as they had a new delivery of vintage dresses arriving in the morning and would have these sorted out by then.

All of them then discussed Murdo's runway plans, the music, and other aspects including the catering and dancing after the show.

'Ean, Innis and I have been discussing the catering,' said Finlay. 'The ticket sales are fantastic, so we're going to have a packed audience for the actual fashion show. We'd thought that moving the dining tables to the edges of the function room would suffice to allow seats to be lined up for people to watch the models walk down the runway. But with the capacity at full for the audience, we need more room for seating, so Ean suggested we erect a marquee in the castle gardens where guests can enjoy something to eat and drink.'

'A marquee?' Skye exclaimed. 'That would be wonderful.'

'And expensive surely,' said Holly, not wanting to bring things down to cost.

'The castle will put the marquee up at our expense,' Ean told them.

'But that's not fair on you,' Holly reasoned.

'It's minimal cost in the grand scheme of things,' Ean explained, fudging the issue. 'We will benefit from promoting the castle and functions, including the ability to hire a marquee for a wedding for example.'

This made sense to the others, but Ean and Finlay glanced at Murdo, urging him not to say anything.

Murdo kept his lips sealed until he saw Rory striding in.

Rory walked up to Murdo. 'I've got the wood you ordered for the new runway outside in the van. Where do you want me to put it?'

'The old new wood that you don't need,' Murdo said to Rory, urging him to go along with the ruse.

Rory blinked. 'Eh, yes, a few planks that I've cut to size for you.' He sounded hesitant, but smiled at Ailsa, Skye and Holly. 'Evening ladies.'

They nodded acknowledgment to Rory.

'I'll help you take it round the back to the castle's storeroom,' said Murdo.

Rory lingered. 'Are you having a dress rehearsal for the fashions?'

'No, we're having a meeting to discuss the show,' Ean told Rory.

'Oh, I wondered, seeing you ladies wearing such lovely dresses,' Rory remarked to the women.

'We just wanted to dress up in vintage for the meeting,' Ailsa explained to Rory.

'Well, you're looking very beautiful,' said Rory, aiming his comment at Ailsa and smiling at her.

Ailsa felt a blush form across her cheeks at the strength of Rory's compliment.

'Thank you, Rory,' she said.

'Excuse me, Ean,' Geneen said, hurrying in. 'One of the guests is eager to talk to you about your paintings in reception. Would you have a moment to chat to them?'

'Yes,' Ean said, and walked away with Geneen.

He could hear Rory chatting to Ailsa, and felt his heart twist in the wind.

'Come on, Rory,' Murdo urged him. 'Let's get that wood put away in the storeroom. Drive your van round to the back of the castle. I'll open up and we'll make short work of it, so you can head home. I didn't know you'd deliver it personally tonight.'

'It was no bother,' Rory told Murdo. And a fine excuse to drop by the castle. Everyone had been talking about the fashion show and he'd heard that Ailsa and the others were meeting there. Rory looked at Skye. 'Lyle told me you're looking for men to walk with the models during part of the show. Put my name down, if you think I'm suitable.'

Skye smiled brightly. 'We'll definitely put you on the list, Rory, but you'll have to be prepared to take part in dress rehearsals.'

'I'm up for that,' Rory assured her.

Cambeul spoke up. 'Can I have your name so I can include it in the feature?'

Rory and Cambeul were introduced, and Rory gave the journalist his name and explained that he was a builder with no modelling experience, but was looking forward to joining his cousin, Lyle, and Brodrick, on the runway with the models.

Murdo took charge, and swept Rory away. As they walked through reception towards the front door, Murdo smiled and nodded at Ean. A less than subtle gesture that he'd taken Rory away from chatting up the ladies, at least until Ean was with them again.

CHAPTER SIX

'Finlay and Ean don't want the ladies out of pocket for the wee extras needed for the fashion show,' Murdo told Rory as they took the wood from the van into the storeroom.

'Ah, okay.' Rory understood to keep his mouth shut.

They put the last pieces of wood in the storeroom. It was near the kitchen area where Innis was making his sweets and the scent of chocolate wafted in the air.

'Do you want a hand to knock the runway together?' Rory offered.

'Have you got the time? I know you're busy with your building work.'

'Ach, I'm always busy. But if I'm going to be one of the models, I should muck in and do my bit.'

Murdo eyed him. 'As long as you're not using it as an excuse to chat up the lassies.'

'I'll be on my best behaviour.'

'Aye, that's what I'm worried about,' Murdo said, half joking.

Rory laughed. 'I might have a wee fancy for Ailsa, but...'

'Don't go treading on Ean's hopes,' Murdo warned him.

'I'm the bold type. Ean's not. But why should I have to wait until he's ready to ask Ailsa out on a date? What if she says no to him?'

'Folk think she likes Ean. She's just as shy as him. And she's been away a lot. They haven't had a chance to get properly acquainted again,' Murdo reasoned.

'Fair enough. But I'm not the only one with his eye on Ailsa. I saw the way Cambeul was looking at her.'

Murdo had too. 'Ailsa's a beautiful young woman. She's bound to get lots of attention.'

'Skye and Holly were looking gorgeous as well,' said Rory. 'Maybe I'll get to walk one of them down the runway. Skye seemed happy to add me to their list, so perhaps I'll get to walk with her.'

Innis walked into the full force of Rory's comment. The aroma of chocolate and vanilla filled the air along with a sense of tension.

'I heard someone in the storeroom at this time of night,' Innis said, explaining why he'd come in to check what was going on.

'Rory's helping me with building the runway,' Murdo explained.

Innis nodded, unsmiling, and made no comment about Rory's remark. 'I'll get back to making my chocolates.' He then headed away to the kitchen next door to the storeroom.

Rory looked at Murdo.

'I appreciate your help with the runway, Rory, but don't go causing any romantic ructions.'

'Aye, no problem.'

Ean finished talking to the guests about his paintings and made his way back to join Finlay and the others. They were now sitting at their table again. But Ailsa and Cambeul weren't with them.

'Where's Ailsa?' said Ean.

Skye spoke up. 'She popped through to the kitchen to talk to her uncle. He's helping Innis make chocolates, and Cambeul went with her. He said he wanted to see Innis' chocolatier work.'

Ean smiled his thanks to Skye. 'I'll be back shortly,' he said, and then headed through to the castle kitchen.

Innis commandeered an area of the kitchen for making his chocolates. Boxes of the delicious confectionery were piled up on one of the counters, and the air was rich with the aroma of chocolate, vanilla, strawberry and other flavours.

Cambeul was eating one of the truffles that was rolled in chocolate flakes and mumbling about how tasty it was.

Cambeul scribbled in his notepad:

Innis, chocolatier. Delicious sweets made in castle kitchen.

Hearing Ailsa chat to her uncle, Cambeul noted:

Ailsa's uncle — castle head chef.

Cambeul had added to his earlier notes:

Rory — builder, walking with models at fashion show.

Ailsa's uncle assisted Innis to make the chocolates, but they'd almost made enough and were starting to clear up for the night.

'Could I take a few pictures of you doing your chocolatier work, with Ailsa standing in the scene wearing that lovely vintage tartan dress?' Cambeul said to Innis.

Innis nodded, and Cambeul adjusted where Ailsa was standing, creating a scene that showed the dress she was wearing in the castle's kitchen and the array of chocolates being made by Innis.

Ean came into the kitchen just in time to see Ailsa posing for the photographs.

Cambeul took the photos and then noticed Ean standing there wearing his kilt and invited Ean to join in.

'I need a kiltie to complement Ailsa's Scottish vintage look,' Cambeul explained.

Seeing Ailsa smile at him, Ean stepped close to her and agreed to be included in the pictures, aware that these could be in the magazine.

Ean stood beside Ailsa, and Cambeul pictured them together.

'Perfect,' said Cambeul. 'I'll send these off to Celia. She'll love this Scottish tartan look. I know your kilt isn't vintage, Ean, but the whole scene is ideal.'

Ailsa peered at the pictures and nodded. 'These are great.' She smiled at Ean and he felt his heart squeeze. 'You look so handsome in your kilt.'

Cambeul finished by taking pictures with all three of them included, with Innis wearing his chef's whites but still looking every part the handsome wolf.

Leaving Innis to get on with finishing his work, Ean, Ailsa and Cambeul headed back to the function room where the dancing had tempted Skye and Holly to join in. Finlay danced with them in a popular reel.

Skye saw Ailsa and beckoned her to join them.

Ailsa glanced at Ean and Cambeul wondering if they'd all join in the dancing.

Cambeul hesitated. 'I don't know the steps.'

'It doesn't matter,' Ailsa told him. 'Just join in the fun.'

She clasped hands with Cambeul and Ean, and they joined in the fast–moving reel, whirling around the dance floor.

Cambeul went to step out of the dancing when the reel finished, but was pulled straight into the next dance, ensuring he had a fun workout and a taste of the island's hospitality.

The night wore on in a blaze of dancing, refreshments, chatter and laughter, and as the evening drew to a close with a slow waltz, Innis arrived in time, having changed out of his chef's whites, into his kilt, to see Ean ask Ailsa to dance with him. She happily accepted, while Cambeul sat down at the table and drank a glass of whisky, scribbling more notes.

One of the guests was dancing with Holly, and Skye was at the buffet having an ice cream lemonade drink.

Innis approached her, taking her aback when he said over her shoulder, 'Would you like to dance with me?'

Skye smiled and put her drink down, and let Innis lead her on to the floor.

Taking her in hold, they started to dance, waltzing past Ean and Ailsa.

'They'd make a great couple,' Skye said to Innis.

Innis nodded thoughtfully. 'They would.'

'But I don't think Ailsa's ready for romance yet,' Skye added.

'Why not?'

'She dated her ex–boyfriend for years. She's said she wants time to herself, at least for a few months.'

'Didn't she split with her ex at New Year?'

'She did. Maybe that's long enough,' Skye relented. 'But she's been away a lot doing her modelling. She told us she wants time to relax at home in her cottage. I don't blame her. It's one of the loveliest cottages on the island.'

'Has she ever mentioned about settling down?'

'Not really, but she doesn't want to move away from the island. She enjoys her crafts and wants to build up her craft shop. The knitting bee members have all helped keep her shop ticking over when she's been away. But she said to us that she's not doing any more modelling jobs for a wee while.'

'Hopefully, this will give her a chance to be more settled,' he said.

Skye looked up at Innis, so tall as he held her in his arms as they danced. 'What about you? Do you like living in the castle or would you prefer a wee house of your own? You've got your cake shop. You're the only brother with his own business, apart from helping to run the castle.'

His guts twisted, torn more these days, longing to settle down, and yet nowhere near having the ability to do so. He wanted in that moment to pull Skye closer to him, but he didn't. The slow waltz offered the perfect chance to feel what his life could be like with Skye in it. The woman he'd known since she'd arrived back at the island, a young lady, along with Holly, taking over the vintage dress shop.

'Your thoughts are an ocean away.'

Skye's words broke into his wayward thoughts and his amber eyes gazed down at her. 'I was just thinking about your question. How to answer it.'

'Perhaps that's your answer. You just don't know.'

Nodding, he waltzed her around the room, until the music faded and the night came to a close.

Ailsa drove Skye and Holly home.

'What was Ean saying to you when you were dancing?' Skye said to Ailsa. She sat in the back seat while Holly sat in the front.

'I asked him about his hill running, and he was talking about that. And about the fashion show.'

'Nothing lovey–dovey?' Holly prompted her.

'No, there's no chance of that when we're whirling around doing the reels,' said Ailsa. 'The last dance of the night always seems too short to have a proper conversation about...romance.'

'How do you feel about him?' Holly added.

'I don't know,' said Ailsa. 'I think I'm holding back from getting involved again if I'm honest. And in the past few months I've seen Ean become more mature, and I like that.'

'He's very handsome, don't you think?' said Skye.

'Yes, he is,' Ailsa agreed.

Before they could discuss this any longer, Ailsa pulled the car up outside the vintage dress shop, and they all went inside to change out of their party dresses.

'I'll put the kettle on for tea,' said Holly. 'Do you want a cup?' she said to Ailsa.

'I've an early start in the morning,' said Ailsa. 'I think I'll head home before I get too tired.'

'Thanks for coming to the meeting tonight,' Skye said to Ailsa, and gave her a hug.

Smiling, Ailsa left the vintage dress shop, waved to her friends, and drove up the hill to her cottage. She'd inherited it the previous year from her grandmother, when her gran moved to Edinburgh to stay with her sister. Twinkle lights were draped around the door, anchored by the wayward wisteria. Climbing roses clambered up the whitewashed walls, and the late summer blooms were being overtaken by autumn florals and the sunflowers in her garden were her current favourite.

She parked her car and stepped out into the garden that was fragrant with night–scented flowers. The twinkle lights were set on a timer and illuminated the cottage with a welcoming glow.

Inside, the cottage had retained the heat of the day and felt cosy as she got ready for bed. Situated on the hillside above the main street, she had a view of the harbour and the sea from her bedroom window. The best view in the world.

Gazing out at the shimmering sea and the stars twinkling like the fairy lights around her front door, she thought about Ean.

Since she'd split with her ex at New Year, her feelings for Ean had become stronger, and now that it was autumn, the depths of her interest had increased until she wondered if she was in jeopardy of falling deeply in love with him. For her heart would be in danger of being broken if their relationship amounted to nothing more than familiarity and friendship rather than true love. And yet...Ean had changed from being the youngest of the three brothers living in the castle, to a fine and handsome young man. People considered Ean to be an amiable character, and he was, but when his emerging manliness and strength was added to the mix, it created a recipe for romantic potential that was excitingly potent.

'What was Innis saying to you tonight?' Holly said to Skye as they drank their tea and tidied up the dress shop, ready for the delivery of more vintage dresses in the morning.

Skye switched on the computer to check the orders while she replied. 'We were talking about Ean and Ailsa. They looked like a couple this evening when they were dancing at the end of the night.'

'They weren't the only ones,' Holly's green eyes shot a knowing look across the rails of dresses to her sister.

Skye caught it and then focussed on the number of orders that had come in since they'd been at the castle. The screen lit up her surprised but delighted face. 'We've had a ton of orders.'

'Luckily we've more dresses being delivered,' said Holly, and then reversed the conversation back to what she wanted to talk about. 'I saw the way Innis was looking at you when you were dancing.'

Skye glanced up from viewing the orders. 'Okay, so he did hold me a wee bit closer than usual, as if he liked me.'

'You've always fancied him,' Holly reminded her.

'I have, or I did. But in the summertime I seemed to come to my senses and realised a man like Innis, that most women lust after, is never going to fall for me. I'm not the serious type, and he totally is.'

'The perfect foil for each other,' Holly suggested.

'Oh, yes. I'll drive him spare with my silliness. And he'll flatten my enthusiasm for frivolities.'

'Or you'll lighten his mood when he's dour. And he'll tame the wild streak in you.'

'Maybe I like being a wee bit wild sometimes.'

Holly shrugged and continued to hang up the dresses. 'Love could still find a way.'

'Perhaps, but it'll have a twisty–turny road to get there. And I certainly don't feel like going down the romance rabbit hole right now, not when we're in the whirlwind of publicity and promoting our shop.'

Holly was inclined to agree. 'Keep your feelings for Innis on the back burner, for now, but don't let the heat fizzle out.'

'I won't. But someone else could snap up Innis. There's always someone new arriving off the ferry. Look at Elspeth and Merrilees.' They were the perfect example. 'He could fall for a beautiful city girl.'

'Not if he really likes you, and that's the look I saw from him tonight,' said Holly.

'Innis' emotions run so deep it makes it hard to read his true feelings.'

'Give him time,' Holly advised her. 'Ean has matured recently and probably Innis has too, and he'll maybe be starting to think of settling down. With Finlay looking set to be with Merrilees, it could put

Innis in the notion of finding romance on the island. Even lone wolf types fall in love.'

Skye nodded thoughtfully, and then continued to process the orders ready for the morning before they headed home.

Ean and Finlay sat outside on the patio at the back of the castle, unwinding after a hectic day and an even more chaotic evening.

Innis joined them, bringing out a tray of tea from the kitchen. The last thing he'd done before securing the chocolate making area for the night.

He put the tray on the table and sat down with Ean and Finlay.

A vast starry sky arched over the castle grounds and the warrior trees, silhouetted against the dark blue, looked strong, refusing to let their guard down. Something Ean was mirroring. He knew what it felt like to have his heart skewered and fried when it came to romance. Almost marrying a young woman from the mainland a couple of years ago had taught him that. She hadn't been the one for him, but that didn't dilute the strength of the feelings he'd had for her. Now long gone.Ean had looked set to marry first. Now his money was on Finlay putting an engagement ring on Merrilees finger soon, followed by a band of wedding gold. The oldest, by three years, Finlay was in line to marry first. And Ean was happy for his brother. Now Ean had to deal with his growing feelings for Ailsa.

But Ean was aware that fickleness could come in and scatter his hopes like marbles. Did Ailsa like him as more than a friendly acquaintance?

'Don't mope,' Innis told Ean, pouring three cups of strong tea. 'It doesn't suit you.'

It was on the tip of Ean's tongue to instantly refute this, but then he accepted the truth, he was moping.

'And don't let Cambeul step in and ensnare Ailsa,' Innis added.

'Strong words,' said Ean, taken aback by the realistic intensity. Spoken in the calm air, Innis' tone had the added weight of a dark night.

Innis poured milk in his tea, stirred it and leaned back in his chair, those amber eyes of his viewing Ean with unequal measures of shrewdness and strength. Innis knew fine that Ean had fallen for Ailsa. The question was, how far, how deep...?

'Rory likes Ailsa too,' said Ean.

'He has a lot of confidence in himself,' Finlay remarked.

'I ran past his house last week,' Ean told them. 'You should see it these days.'

Innis frowned. 'The old house in the middle of nowhere?'

'It might be in the middle of nowhere, surrounded by green fields and heather, but you should see it now. It was a ramshackle when Rory bought it for sweetie money a couple of years ago. The building work needed was huge. Practically just a strong shell with no roof. I'd never run that route these past years or so. But he's built himself a fine mansion and cultivated a garden with a summerhouse,' said Ean.

'The builder in him has come in handy,' Finlay commented.

'And the determination to do it,' Ean added.

'So he's got a steady building business, he's young, around the same age as us, no baggage, and an impressive house in the heart of the island,' Finlay noted.

Ean nodded. 'He has a friendly, outgoing nature too. And a confident attitude when it comes to chatting up the ladies.'

'Spark up some of that for yourself,' Innis told Ean.

'Easier said than done.' Ean's tone was dour.

'Is it?' said Innis. 'If you like Ailsa, start bucking up and stop moping. The doldrums isn't a good look when it comes to romance.'

Ean sighed heavily. 'It'll be a challenge.'

'Merrilees was a challenge,' Finlay told Ean. 'She still is, but it keeps our relationship exciting.'

'I'd happily settle for calm and cosy,' said Ean.

'Win her heart first,' Finlay told Ean. 'Then you can have cosy.'

Many a night when Ean had been out running in the summertime along the shore, he'd looked up at Ailsa's cottage on the hillside, windows aglow and with twinkle lights sparkling in the darkle. There was cosy and contentment.

A wave of energy washed through him. It was time to fight for Ailsa. But not right in the midst of the fashion show and the promotion deal with Cambeul and the magazine feature. The castle would take centre stage in the magazine during the show. The vintage dress shop would do likewise when the fashions were highlighted. He needed to find a way to keep things on an even keel for a few days until the night of the show.

Finishing their tea, the brothers headed upstairs to the private part of the castle where they each had their own accommodation. Finlay's suite had the added benefit of access to one of the turrets. Ean didn't mind. He liked being tucked into the back of the castle with a balcony offering a view of the gardens, forest beyond and the vast sky.

A silvery moon shone in the distance, creating a magical quality to the night as he stood there, stripped down to his cream silk pyjama bottoms, feeling the air waft against his bare chest.

His shoulders had broadened over the past year, and he could feel the muscles in his torso more toned than ever from all the running, hard work, busy lifestyle and maturity. He'd become the man he'd always had the potential to be. Now the only thing missing from his world was true and lasting love, hopefully with Ailsa.

CHAPTER SEVEN

Ailsa was up early and ate breakfast in her cottage kitchen. She'd painted it yellow earlier in the year and loved the sunshine effect it created. Her teapot had a bumblebee tea cosy that Primrose had knitted for her. It had a small, knitted bumble on the top of it. And Rosabel had knitted her pretty egg cosies.

Her busy day started after breakfast. And later it was the knitting bee night. Fired up on a bowl of porridge and a cup of tea, she went through to the living room she'd adapted as an overspill from her craft shop she leased to sell various crafts — jewellery, knitted shawls, hats and scarves, watercolour prints of the island, craft kits and art materials like the paints Ean had bought.

Morning sunlight streamed through the back window of the living room, highlighting the crafter's paradise she'd created. Shelves were filled with her fabric stash for quilting, balls of yarn for knitting and crochet, embroidery thread, crewel wool, cross stitched patterns and tapestry items, along with glass jars of beads and gems that she used for her jewellery making. Pretty necklaces, bangles and bracelets hung from a carousel. Watercolours were framed on the walls. None of them painted by Ean. But perhaps she could buy one from him. She really did love his artwork.

An embroidery hoop had an autumn theme pattern she'd been working on that had acorns, chestnut leaves, little pumpkins and chocolate daisies in the design. It was half finished. She tucked it in her craft bag to take to the shop and work on between packing up the online orders and taking them to the post office, something she did most days. Her online sales dominated her business, but she liked having an actual shop, like an anchor on the island along with the cottage itself.

She wore a knee–length, flare, red tartan skirt, a vintage piece that Holly and Skye let her purloin while helping them put the slower selling items in their shop's storeroom. A long sleeve, hand knitted red jumper, that always gave her a boost of bright energy, suited her pale complexion and dark hair. Wearing black pumps, she picked up her craft bag and headed out to start her day at the craft shop.

Dazzling sunshine shone in a cloudless cobalt sky. Ailsa squinted across at the calm sea that reflected the sky, giving the upper hand to the blue hue of the deep, blue–green sea.

The main street shops and all along the harbour and up into the hills looked like summer was at its height, as if someone had forgotten to give the island the memo that it was now autumn.

Pretty bunting fluttered in the light breeze outside Ailsa's shop and others, including the vintage dress shop.

Her front window display was an eclectic mix of crafting enticements, lit up by the sun shining on them.

Ailsa was about to put the key in the lock when she heard someone call to her.

'We have iced doughnuts!' Skye shouted to Ailsa.

Dropping the keys back in her bag, Ailsa walked along to the vintage dress shop shaking her head at Skye. 'You are such a bad influence.'

'Come and have a rummage through the pile of new vintage dresses that have just arrived. We. Are. Swooning.'

Ailsa was used to Skye over–egging her descriptions, but this time she wasn't exaggerating. 'Wow! Just wow!'

'Aren't they gorgeous,' Holly enthused, holding up one of the dresses — a fairytale evening dress, tulle and silk in white, shot through with gold threads. And then showing Ailsa a beige and bronze baroque style dress with a gem encrusted bodice flowing down to a full–length cascade of sparkling chiffon.

There were designer dresses from decades past, along with handcrafted gowns made to measure for the wearer in lace, velvet, watered silk, and every luxurious fabric imaginable.

'This floral silk fabric is out of this world,' Holly said, in awe of the beautiful design.

Three large boxes of dresses had arrived, all carefully packed and pre–cleaned.

'I don't see any that need repaired,' Skye observed.

'You have to include these in the fashion show,' Ailsa insisted.

They took no persuading.

Skye picked up two dresses and clutched them against herself and gazed in the full–length mirror near the little changing room. 'These two are not for sale. Ever.'

No one disagreed.

Ailsa put her bag down and rummaged through the most beautiful collection of vintage dresses she'd seen in a long time. 'Where did you get these?'

'One of our suppliers. They were asked to clear out a large mansion in the Highlands, and these were in the wardrobes. I'm sure some of them have never been worn.'

Ailsa checked the dresses and agreed.

'The fabrics are wonderful,' said Holly.

Ailsa admired the way some of the seams had been stitched, buttons sewn on, a side zip put in. Did the dress have a designer label? Every aspect was a telltale of the dress' history. It was something that fascinated Ailsa, discovering the back story of a dress, who wore it, if anyone, or was it bought and hung for decades in a wardrobe only now seeing the light of day. Pre–loved dresses had a second chance to be loved again. Ailsa loved that connection of the past and the present.

Skye wore a rust brown, fine needle cord, slight flared maxi skirt. The colour was ideal for autumn. With it she wore a skimpy beige vest with a cropped Aran knit cardigan. The top buttons were undone to create a hint of décolletage, while the earthy tones and texture of the cable knit created a stylish blend of rustic and risqué. Slouch faux suede boots completed the look.

Holly's dark denim, button up front, A–line skirt skimmed just below the calves, and she wore it with a navy and red skinny rib jumper with cap sleeves and a lace–up V–neckline. It did wonders for her great figure. Navy T–bar shoes with mid–heels added to the slightly retro slant of the outfit.

Holly and Skye usually wore more dresses than separates, but with lots of the dresses being earmarked for the fashion show and hung on rails, labelled for each part of the show and the names of the ladies modelling them, they'd opted to wear the separates that had been relegated to the storeroom.

'Our suppliers have found a real cache of exquisite dresses,' Holly enthused. She ran her hand gently down a burgundy velvet evening dress with a fitted waistline and flared skirt. 'These are going to be so difficult to part with.' She clutched it to herself and admired it in the mirror.

The kettle clicked off. 'I'll make the tea,' said Skye, heading through to the kitchen. 'I popped into Innis' shop this morning for chocolate scones. Primrose served me, but as I was leaving Innis thrust a bag of iced doughnuts into my hands, knowing I love those.' She made the tea and didn't elaborate on their conversation, but it was so unexpected for Innis to do this. Often she'd go in and he'd barely acknowledge her, though lately he'd been more amicable.

'Here, take these,' he'd said to her. 'For good behaviour.'

She'd accepted the delicious doughnuts. 'Thank you, Innis, but I can't promise I'll be well behaved.'

'That's fine. I can live with that.' His amber eyes looked at her as he said this, causing her heart to react.

'Help yourself to a doughnut,' Holly said to Ailsa as they joined Skye in the kitchen.

Skye blinked from her thoughts of her encounter with Innis, and then tried not to read too much into it.

'Sticky doughnuts and tea are banned from the front shop,' Skye reminded them, including herself in this rule. 'Until those gorgeous dresses are properly sorted and hung on the rails, and even then, I wouldn't risk it until we've worn them to the fashion show.'

'I don't know about you,' Holly said to Ailsa, 'but we slept sound. We almost slept in.' She held up her doughnut. 'This is breakfast. We didn't have time to cook anything.'

'I slept well, probably tuckered out from all the excitement,' said Ailsa.

'From the fashion show, or from Ean?' Skye teased her.

'Or Rory,' Holly added.

'You are soooo spoiled for choice,' Skye said to Ailsa.

Ailsa sipped her tea and ate her doughnut, and smiled, not taking them up on their teasing.

Skye cupped her tea and looked at Ailsa. 'If you had to go on a date with one of them. Would it be Ean? Or Rory?'

'What about Cambeul?' said Holly.

'He's leaving in a week,' said Skye. 'We're talking about boyfriend potential.'

Giggling, they continued to enjoy their tea and doughnuts and chat about romance and vintage dresses.

Ean ran across the field at speed. He wore black training gear and looked like a fast–moving silhouette in the morning mist that wafted over the grass and heather covered field in the middle of nowhere on the island.

The early morning dew, mixed with the warmth of the day, had yet to be burned off by the sunlight. It created a haze across the landscape that Ean had all to himself. There was a dreamlike quality to the scenery, and as he ran across a large patch of white heather, he wondered if it would bring him luck today. No sooner had the thought crossed his mind, than he pushed the notion aside. Luck wasn't on his mind. Only the determined intention of asking Ailsa out on a date filled his thoughts.

With this in mind, he ran like the wind, faster and faster, as the sun highlighted his dark silhouette before he disappeared into the rising mist of the distant hills.

Shuggie dropped off his first fare of the morning at the front entrance of the castle. As he was about to drive away, Cambeul came running out, waving him down. He had one of the castle's bags that he'd stuffed with a towel and a few other items.

'Are you available for hire?'

'Yes, hop in.'

Checking that there wasn't a cat on the passenger seat, Cambeul sat up front with Shuggie as they drove away from the castle.

'Where are you off to?' said Shuggie.

'The shore. I'm taking you up on your idea that I should go swimming. Any suggestions for the best locations for this on the island.'

'My favourite cove. It's near the far end of the harbour. The water there is clear and deep. Great for a dook.'

Cambeul settled back in his seat. 'Let's head there.'

Ailsa managed to pry herself away from the vintage dresses and head to her craft shop to get on with her work.

After dealing with the orders, she picked up the autumn theme embroidery she was working on, and sat calmly, enjoying satin stitching the acorns with single strands of copper and bronze coloured cotton embroidery thread, and gazed out the window at the sunny day.

A message came through on her phone from Elspeth at the knitting shop, reminding her that their usual knitting bee evening was being used to organise things for the fashion show, including rehearsing how to do model–like turns on the runway.

You're expertise will be needed, Ailsa. Hope you can come along to the bee.

I'll be there. Happy to help.

Ean arrived back at the castle and walked through reception, heading upstairs to shower and change out of his training gear.

He met Finlay on his way to the function room.

'I know there's a party night on this evening,' said Ean. 'But I'm planning to go to Ailsa's cottage tonight. Can you manage the party without me?'

'Ah,' said Finlay. 'She won't be in. The knitting bee night has been moved to this evening so the ladies can start organising themselves for the fashion show.'

'Right.' The disappointment sounded in Ean's voice.

'And in case you're thinking of popping along to the knitting bee to chat to her, Cambeul told me this morning that he's been invited to attend so he can interview some of the ladies.'

Ean sighed wearily. 'Thanks for letting me know.' He started to head up the stairs.

'Don't let this put you off your plans. Find another way to talk to Ailsa,' Finlay said to him.

Ean nodded and forced a smile, feeling thwarted yet again from asking Ailsa to have dinner with him.

'One more length of the shore, Cambeul!' Shuggie shouted to him. 'You can do it.'

Shuggie relaxed on the sand, leaning back on a grassy dune, while Cambeul swam along the coast. Nettie had made him a flask of tea to take with him. He poured himself a cup, and dunked a shortcake and raisin biscuit in his tea, feeling exhausted just watching Cambeul going for it.

'You're a hard taskmaster,' Cambeul tried to shout back, but some of his words were watery splutters.

Shuggie heard him fine, but pretended otherwise. 'Go on yerself, Cambeul.'

Celia sat in her office and looked at the pictures Cambeul had sent to her.

Seona brought in Celia's latte and sat it down on her desk.

Celia pointed to her computer screen. 'These pics are perfect.'

'There's Innis making his chocolates. Oooh! delicious. And the chocolates look tasty too.'

Celia iced her with a look.

'Sorry, I'm just joking. But seriously, that tartan dress looks amazing.'

'It's the ideal intro for our Scottish vintage piece. Ailsa is modelling it.'

Seona eyed the pictures. 'Who is the handsome kiltie?'

'Ean.'

Seona admired him, and then was distracted by the sweets. 'Tell Cambeul to send us a box of those chocolates.'

Celia pushed a box of them across the desk. 'Compliments of the castle. They posted them out when the booking was made.'

'Can I have one?'

'Help yourself.' A few were already missing.

'I'll grab my coffee.' Seona ran out to get her cappuccino from her desk.

Celia popped another chocolate truffle in her mouth and started to plan the vintage fashion feature around the photographs.

Cambeul finally emerged from the sea and walked up on to the sand towards where Shuggie was relaxing.

Cambeul went to reach for his towel to dry himself off and sit down, but Shuggie remained in coaching mode.

'No, walk up and down a wee bit first, and feel the sand beneath your feet,' Shuggie advised. 'Let the soles of your feet absorb the goodness of the minerals in the sand.'

Cambeul frowned, dubious, but went along with it and then felt the relaxing benefit of walking on the sand, minerals or not.

Shuggie unscrewed the other cup on the flask and poured Cambeul a cup of tea.

'Here you go.' Shuggie handed it to him and topped up his own cup. 'Do you want a squashed fly to go with it?'

Cambeul sat down on his towel and was glad of the cuppa. 'Yes, give me one.'

Shuggie gave him one of the biscuits, and they sat in the morning sunlight, gazing out at the glistening sea, and exchanging gossip.

Finally, Cambeul stood up and brushed the sand from himself. He was about to put on his clothes when Shuggie stopped him.

'Nah! You've not finished your training yet. Put your towel on the car seat. We're heading to the waterfall on the way back to the castle. It's not far.'

'Waterfall? More swimming?'

'Aye and naw. Come on. You can't come to the island without experiencing a dip in the waterfall.'

Going along with Shuggie's suggestion, Cambeul kept his swimming trunks on, sat on his towel and they drove away from the shore into the forest.

'They call it forget–me–not waterfall because of all the wee blue flowers growing around it,' Shuggie explained as he manoeuvred off the forest road into a narrower route that led them to a place that appeared out from the dense trees in a niche and looked like an enchanted waterfall with lots of flowers and greenery.

Shuggie parked the car. 'Great, you've got it to yourself. In you go.'

Needing little encouragement, Cambeul walked across the lush grass and greenery and stepped over the emerald moss covered edge of the main pool into the water.

'Oh, it's a bit cold,' Cambeul said, but was fascinated by how clear the water was.

'The water is always naturally clear as crystal,' Shuggie explained, standing at the edge. 'But that's not the main reason why we're here.' He glanced up at the water teaming down overhead. The sound as it rushed over the tipping point and fell down into the pool below, indicated the force of it.

Cambeul hesitated. 'You want me to stand under it?' He looked dubious. 'Is this some sort of ancient island challenge?'

'You wanted to keep up your training. This is your cool down,' Shuggie told him. 'Under you go. See if you can last for one to two minutes. I'll time you.'

Cambeul shook his arms and legs, getting himself keyed up. 'I'm betting the water is cold.'

'That's a fair bet.' Shuggie got his phone ready to capture the antics.

Taking a deep breath, Cambeul stepped under the waterfall and gasped as the cold water drowned out his initial yelling. Then he seemed to become energised, and through the torrent started to laugh as Shuggie shouted the time.

'One minute! On, ye go, Cambeul!'

'I'm going for the full two minutes!' Cambeul shouted but his voice was tempered by the force of the downpour.

Cambeul was laughing and challenging himself, loving every second of it.

'Thirty second to go,' Shuggie called to him.

Cambeul knew he had this in the bag, and stood defiant, letting the cold water bounce off his chest as he arched back and let it pour over his face.

'Times up!' Shuggie shouted.

Cambeul steeled himself to last another few seconds, before stepping out from under the waterfall and wading across the pool towards Shuggie.

Shuggie started clapping. 'Impressive stuff.'

'I thoroughly enjoyed that.' Cambeul stepped out of the pool and shook the residue of water off.

'That's the best I've seen from a newcomer,' Shuggie told him.

'Do I get a medal?' Cambeul said jokingly.

'No, but you get a hot cup of tea and a shower back at the castle. Will that do?'

'It will, Shuggie. And thanks for pushing me to do it.'

Shuggie checked the photos he'd taken and a short video clip. 'I'll send a copy to your phone.' He showed Cambeul a sample of the photos.

'These are going straight to Celia,' Cambeul announced. 'Seona will be glad she got the designer handbag.'

Shuggie frowned.

'Never mind,' said Cambeul. 'This will brighten their day.'

'Seona!' Celia called from her office, sounding as if something urgent had happened.

Rushing in, Seona saw that Celia eyeballs were glued to her computer screen watching something with great interest.

Before Seona could say anything, Celia pointed and said, 'Take a look at what's just popped through on my email.'

Seona's eyes widened. 'I didn't know Cambeul was...built.'

From the expression on Celia's face, neither did she.

'Where is he?'

'Forget–me–not waterfall, on the island. It's near the castle. Apparently, an acquaintance he's made challenged him.'

Seona looked at the swimming trunks he was wearing — a pair of red tartan shorts. 'Are you thinking what I'm thinking?'

Celia gave a conspiratorial smile. 'Oh, yes.'

CHAPTER EIGHT

'A picture of me in the fashion feature?' Cambeul sounded aghast as he took the call from Celia. 'Beside my byline. Wearing tartan swimming trunks.'

'It would be really great for the opening Scottish fashion feature,' said Celia. 'Showing the journalist who went to the island to cover the show, and jumped in at the deep end of the waterfall. The pics are very flattering.'

This was the first time Celia had ever acknowledged that Cambeul was fit and quite athletic looking.

'You've been hiding your assets under your cargo trousers and beige casuals,' Seona called to him, joining in the conversation.

'Okay, I'll play,' Cambeul agreed. His usual byline and feature headline picture was due an overhaul. His current photo showed a head and shoulder shot of him looking editorially smart but unsmiling. And wearing beige.

Ailsa's day had been busy with extra online orders that she needed to parcel up and take to the post office. Loaded with two bags full of craft items wrapped and labelled, she put up a sign in her shop: *Closed until tomorrow*.

Locking the door, she walked the short distance to the post office and dropped off the parcels, and then headed to the knitting shop to talk to Elspeth and Morven about the knitting bee night — mainly how to arrange the room at the back of the knitting shop where the bee evenings were held, so that she could teach the ladies how to walk down the runway for the forthcoming show.

Ean didn't see Ailsa disappear into the knitting shop, that was near her craft shop, as he drove along the main street and parked his car. Dressed smartly in dark trousers and a white pin–stripe shirt, open at the neck, he walked up to the craft shop, going over in his mind what he was going to say to her, to ask her to have dinner with him.

As he approached the shop he read the notice, and halted, his senses jolted once again into disappointment. He glanced around in the hope that she was nearby, but he couldn't see her. He pulled out his phone, but then thought better of it. If she'd closed the shop she had a reason, somewhere to be. This wasn't the moment he was hoping for. Resigned to being scuppered again, he went back to his car and drove home to the castle.

The pretty pink knitting shop had the front door propped open to let in the warm sea air. The shelves were stacked with a wonderful selection of yarn — from double knit to Aran, along with local hand spun varieties. It was sandwiched between Innis' cake shop and Brodrick's cafe bar. Next door to the cake shop was the vintage dress shop. Ailsa's craft shop was nearby, creating a busy hub where their businesses thrived.

Elspeth, thirty, wore her blonde hair in a ponytail and her cornflower blue eyes were filled with interest as Ailsa suggested how to organise the bee night.

'Instead of having all the tables like we usually have for our knitting bee evenings, keep the main part of the floor clear so we can practise the techniques,' said Ailsa. 'Skye and Holly will be helping too.'

Elspeth's Aunt Morven, a very attractive woman in her fifties, nodded in agreement. 'I've spoken to all the ladies who are taking part in the fashion show, including Rosabel and Primrose, and they're keen to learn how to walk on the runway.'

Elspeth lived with her aunt above the knitting shop in the traditional, two–storey, converted cottage that had an extension at the rear of the premises where the knitting bee nights were held. Morven was dating Donall, a strapping man in his fifties. He owned half of a small whisky distillery and was part owner of two of the local pubs. Elspeth's romance with Brodrick was becoming stronger, having started dating him in the late spring, and they'd become quite an established couple on the island. Elspeth was often to be found having dinner at Brodrick's cafe bar or at his house up on the hillside near Ailsa's cottage. Hints of an impending engagement between Elspeth and Brodrick were often part of the gossipmongering, but based on reasonable probability.

'Some members will be bringing their knitting, sewing or other crafts, and they're welcome to do that while we organise ourselves for the fashion. Most members are joining in and helping at the show,' Elspeth explained.

'You can feel the excitement building,' said Ailsa. 'The meeting at the castle last night went well, and there's going to be a marquee set up in the castle grounds for the catering. So many tickets have been sold.'

'It's going to be a popular event,' Elspeth agreed.

'Skye says they'll have the commentary written as soon as the final selection of dresses has been made,' said Morven. 'It'll give Nettie and me time to practise reading it. I've given talks at knitting bee nights and other craft events, but nothing as grand as this.'

'You have a good speaking voice,' Elspeth told her aunt.

Morven smiled. 'Nettie isn't the least bit nervous, so she'll breeze through it.'

'Your experience in fashion shows is invaluable,' Elspeth said to Ailsa. 'Do you ever get nervous stepping out in front of an audience?'

'Every time,' Ailsa admitted.

Elspeth laughed. 'I just hope I don't trip.'

'You won't, and I've got some tips to make sure you walk with poise and confidence,' said Ailsa.

Ailsa stayed to chat and have a cup of tea with them, and offered insights into the world of fashion and design.

'I don't know about you,' said Elspeth, pouring the tea, 'but we haven't stopped working all morning. We skipped lunch and we're going to have a sandwich. Would you like one? It's just tomato and salad.'

'Yes, please. I'm firing on a bowl of porridge for breakfast, and an iced doughnut Skye gave me.'

'Three salad sarnies coming up,' Elspeth said, running upstairs to their private kitchen to make them.

Skye and Holly had changed out of their separates into classic dresses for their interview with Cambeul.

'He'll probably take photos of us,' said Holly, adjusting the waist of the blue and white polka dot dress she was wearing. Fifties fit and flare dresses were among her favourites and she wore the era well.

Skye's look ranged from twenties flapper numbers that she carried off with ease, to bias–cut, thirties art deco style silk and satin sheath dresses with shoestring straps and low–cut backs that suited her slender figure. An afternoon tea dress was her choice for the interview with Cambeul, and the rose print fabric was bold rather than ditsy.

Equally bold was Skye's attitude towards Cambeul. 'Let's invite him to be one of the men walking the runway at the show.'

'Cambeul?' Holly exclaimed.

'Yes, why not?'

Holly didn't have an immediate excuse.

'He's good looking with a fit build, and seems very confident. Just the type we need for the show,' Skye reasoned.

'Okay,' Holly agreed.

Skye checked the time. 'I'm going to pop to Lyle's tea shop to buy a cake for our afternoon tea. I won't be long.'

Skye hurried away in a flurry of vintage rose print with her long hair hanging around her shoulders in a cascade of strawberry gold waves.

Lyle almost dropped the sponge cake he was placing in a display cabinet. 'You're looking particularly lovely this afternoon, Skye.'

'Thank you, Lyle. I need a cake to impress Cambeul while not being too messy. We're showing him our fashions this afternoon,' Skye explained.

He gestured to a white cardboard cake box filled with a selection of cupcakes, each one iced with a different buttercream topping. 'There's classic chocolate, strawberry and vanilla, bramble, lemon and my new autumn flavours — hazelnut, pumpkin and toffee apple.'

'I'll take a box of those. They look delicious.' Skye paid for them and lifted the box off the counter. 'We have a rehearsal for the fashion show tonight at the knitting bee. We need to learn poise and presentation on the runway. Ailsa is helping us demonstrate what to do.'

'It's so handy that you, Holly and Ailsa have fashion show experience. My customers are very interested in seeing the show.'

'Finlay says the ticket sales are great.'

'Well, I hope Cambeul enjoys the cakes,' said Lyle.

'I'm sure he will.' Skye smiled, and then hurried back to the dress shop.

Holly waved urgently to Skye. 'Shuggie's just dropped Cambeul off — and he's heading this way.'

Skye ran through to the kitchen with the cake box. 'I've bought Lyle's cupcakes. They'll be easier to eat, less messy and no cutting cakes.'

'Hello, Cambeul,' Holly said, welcoming him in.

Skye took a deep breath and walked through calmly, as if she hadn't been racing out buying cakes.

Cambeul wore expensive casuals in light neutral tones, and looked around, nodding. 'I love your shop. And you both look terrific in those dresses.'

'Thank you. Have a browse around,' Holly told him.

He took his notepad out of his laptop bag, sat the bag down on the counter and did just that.

'Crepe de chine, moire silk, taffeta and organza,' he said, expertly identifying the fabrics of the dresses hanging on the rails, and jotting them down on his notepad.

'You certainly know your fabrics,' Skye remarked.

'My parents worked in fashion and I grew up in that world,' he explained. 'I considered working in design, but I didn't have the talent to be part of the cream, so I decided I liked to write about it. A fashion magazine took me on, I worked my way up, and now I work for Celia.'

Summarising his expertise, he continued to browse and named not only the fabrics, but the styles of dresses, the eras and whether they were designer numbers or made–to–measure for a particular person.

'These new dresses that arrived in your shop today, are fantastic,' he said.

'We're including them at the show,' Holly told him.

'You should. Look at this gorgeous satin and chiffon ball gown,' he enthused. 'It's a designer piece.'

'Can we keep you for the rest of the day?' Skye joked. 'We had this load of new dresses delivered and haven't categorised them all yet. With your help, we'd have everything done by the time the kettle boils again.'

Cambeul laughed. 'I've a habit of tearing through work, not wasting time, as I work to deadlines with the magazine.'

'Would you like to have afternoon tea with us?' Holly said to him.

'We have cake,' Skye added.

'Cake, in that case...' He smiled and chatted to Skye about their suppliers while Holly put the kettle on to boil and set up the kitchen table with cups, plates and napkins.

'This is very cosy, but civilised,' he said when it was time to sit down for tea.

'Help yourself to one of the tea shop cakes,' said Holly while pouring the tea.

'What flavour is that one?' He pointed to one of the cakes.

Skye checked the list that was tucked in the box, matching it to the cake. 'It's pumpkin, one of Lyle's new recipes for autumn.'

Cambeul lifted the cake and took a bite. 'Mmm, there's a bit of spice in this,' he mumbled, enjoying every mouthful.

Skye opted for the toffee apple cupcake, swooning at the sweet flavour and tart apple.

'I'll try his new hazelnut cupcake,' said Holly, biting into it, almost getting the generous topping on her nose.

The three of them laughed and chatted about vintage fashion, fabrics and dresses, until the afternoon faded to tea time.

'I'd better let you get ready for your knitting bee night,' he said, standing up, having enjoyed his afternoon with them.

He phoned for Shuggie to pick him up.

'I'll be there in a few minutes,' said Shuggie.

Cambeul stood outside the vintage dress shop with Holly and Skye. He'd taken photos during the afternoon, but then asked Shuggie to take a picture of him with the ladies standing outside the shop in the amber glow of the approaching golden hour.

Shuggie was happy to oblige and took a few photos before handing the camera back to Cambeul.

'I'll send these to Celia and give her an update,' Cambeul said to Holly and Skye.

Waving him off, they didn't notice Innis watching them from the cake shop window.

He pretended to fuss with one of the iced cakes on display while peering out at them, having seen them chatting to the magazine journalist.

'The girls are looking lovely in their dresses, don't you think,' Primrose called to Innis.

Amber eyes glanced round at her. He nodded.

'Especially Skye,' Rosabel added. 'She really suits that rose tea dress.'

Innis didn't take them up on their insinuation that he was jealous of Cambeul. He wasn't. There was nothing to be jealous about. Cambeul wasn't dating Skye, and even if he was, what business was it of his.

Not convincing himself in the slightest that this didn't bother him, he admired Skye standing in the mellow sunlight talking animatedly to Holly before they both went inside their shop.

Ean's suite at the back of the castle had an extra room with a small balcony overlooking the gardens and forest beyond. He'd created an artist's studio there, and he had a table set up so he could work on his paintings, watercolour and oils, along with another table that had all his paints and brushes on hand for his artwork.

After being disappointed that he hadn't been able to talk to Ailsa, he'd headed back to the castle and helped Finlay deal with the guests until the late afternoon. Then he'd gone up to his room to relax before having to work in the evening, along with Finlay, at the party night. Most evenings at the castle there was dancing or a party and buffet for guests, so his nights were filled with work as well as play.

Ean's favourite way to relax was to paint, so rather than sleep for an hour or so, he'd set up his watercolour paints, including the new ones he'd bought from Ailsa's craft shop, and started work on one of the paintings he had in mind depicting autumn.

Warm, fragrant air wafted in through the open patio doors leading on to the balcony.

Dragonflies flew by and he hoped to capture their colourful beauty in his paintings.

And there were diva moths, with their purple, lilac, pink, turquoise, orange and gold colours, tiny pieces of artwork in themselves.

The view of the gardens and layers of trees in the distance was a mix of fresh greens with bronze, copper and rustic tones of the other trees and greenery that were starting to show how beautiful autumn could be.

Burnished bronze light streamed across the landscape, and he used watercolour washes of ochre, sienna and umber to create the autumnal tones. Prussian blue, alizarin crimson and other hues were added to the painting as Ean became lost in the process of his artwork. But in his thoughts was Ailsa.

He continued painting until the light faded to early evening, then he showered and got changed into his kilt and went downstairs to help Finlay with the party night.

Rosabel and Primrose were the first to arrive for the knitting bee night.

'We've brought cake,' Rosabel announced, carrying cake boxes through to the back of the shop where Elspeth and Morven had set up the folding chairs while keeping a space on the floor as a practise runway.

'Thank you,' said Morven, leading them through to the kitchen to start making the tea, while Elspeth finished setting up a couple of folding tables along one wall. Sewing machines and fabrics galore were usually set on the tables, but instead there were some of the vintage dresses that Skye had dropped off. Shoes from every decade from the twenties to the eighties were in two large boxes tucked under the tables.

Other accessories from hair clasps to beaded necklaces and bracelets were placed on top of a table where the members were due to be encouraged to help themselves to create the right look for the fashion show.

Several members bustled in, and soon the bee night was in full swing and filled with chatter and excitement.

The large storeroom cupboard where the knitting bee night chairs and tables were kept, was being used as a changing room. The giggles from inside the cupboard sounded twice as loud and raucous as those outside it.

'My face is sore laughing,' Nettie said, smiling, and stepped out wearing a forties polka dot dress that had less of a flare design than the fifties polka dot dresses they had available.

Skye assessed the potential of the dress for Nettie.

'Try on something with a bit more razzamatazz, Nettie,' said Skye. 'You've got the figure for one of the cocktail dresses.'

Nettie blinked, as if this had never crossed her mind. 'Okay, I'll go and put on some sequins and sparkle.'

Two other ladies, hearing the conversation, went back into the storeroom and emerged wearing dresses with more dazzle and daring.

Skye had a list of the dresses, what category they were due to be in — by decade or decadence with cotton print tea dresses suitable for wearing during the day vying against opulent gold brocade evening gowns, sequin cocktail dresses and bargain ball gowns made from layers of chiffon, with bead encrusted bodices. The prices of the dresses reflected the categories from ready–to–wear dresses to classic couture.

All the members turned up and some had brought their knitting or embroidery with them, those not walking on the runway, but helping with the hair, makeup and other sundries. Between the chatter, they knitted and stitched, while the ladies learned how to pivot without doing themselves a mischief.

'I've made a pencil sheet of the models' names and what they're wearing,' Skye told the members. 'This will change once you've tried on the dresses allocated to see if they're suitable.'

Ailsa and Holly were walking up and down the floor with the members, teaching them the turns, how to hold their core strong, head up, shoulders back, and reminded them to smile even if they messed up.

'Smile with confidence,' Holly told them. 'Don't signal your disappointment with a frown.'

'No frowns on the runway,' said Skye. 'Unless it's one of the men trying to be hot and moody.'

'Are you ladies decent?' a man called through to them, entering via the knitting shop.

The women looked round and there was Lyle standing there, poised to join them. Rory was with him.

The laughter and chatter stopped.

'Sorry we're late for the dress rehearsal,' Lyle apologised. 'But I was baking cakes for the morning and needed to wait until they were ready before taking them out of the oven.'

Glances shot between the women, and the members then looked to Holly, Skye and Ailsa to deal with the unexpected gentlemen.

Lyle and Rory were smartly dressed. Lyle wore the trousers belonging to a dark suit with a white shirt and silk tie. And it was the first time Ailsa and the others had seen Rory sans denim. He wore a pair of classic black trousers and a white shirt. His tie was sexily pulled down, making him look like he was ready to break a few hearts with his handsome face and fit build.

Lyle matched him in looks and a few of the women were whispering how handsome they were.

The laughter and chatter notched up a couple of levels as the two men joined in the evening.

'I brought cake.' Lyle handed Morven a bag filled with a selection from the tea shop.

'That's very kind of you, Lyle. We're about to have another round of tea, and I'll divide these up amongst the ladies.'

While the kettle boiled and the chatter rose, Ailsa took charge of Rory and showed him how to present himself on the runway.

Skye linked arms with Lyle as they walked. 'Walk strong and steady, and support your lady as she models her dress. The men are walking with the women at the finale, so the audience will already be fired up with excitement. This is the crescendo before the fashion show ends.'

'Got it,' said Lyle, straightening up, making Skye realise how tall he was. Not as tall as Innis or his brothers, but not far off it.

Rory was a match for the brothers in height, and as the women viewed the builder dressed to impress them, they realised that he was a fine looking man.

'I didn't know there was a dress rehearsal until you told me in the tea shop this afternoon,' Lyle said to Skye. 'But I phoned Rory and well...here we are.'

She didn't have the heart to tell him that he hadn't been included in the dress rehearsal at the knitting bee. But the night was benefiting from having Lyle and Rory there to practice walking with them.

While the tea and cake were served, Skye whispered to Ailsa and Holly about what had happened in the tea shop.

'Don't tell him,' said Ailsa. 'Don't tell Rory either.'

Lyle had gone through to the kitchen to help make the tea and cut the cakes. The tea shop chef in him made short work of both.

'He's fast and efficient,' Morven whispered to Elspeth.

Ailsa agreed with them. 'We should invite Lyle to our knitting bee nights and lock him in the kitchen.'

Lyle overheard her and gave her a cheeky grin. 'You can lock me in the kitchen anytime, Ailsa.'

'And me,' another man's voice said, joining them in the kitchen.

They glanced round, and standing there smiling at them was Cambeul.

Ailsa whispered to Skye under her breath. 'We forgot Cambeul was invited to the knitting bee.'

Skye nodded. 'It's going to be an interesting night, because Primrose just said that Ean has pulled up outside the knitting shop.

'Is he coming in to join us?' Ailsa said urgently.

'Nooo. Ean's obviously here to buy a few skeins of yarn,' Skye joked, and then nudged Ailsa. 'Ean's here for you.'

CHAPTER NINE

Rory stepped close to Ailsa and smiled. 'Come on, show me how to walk down the runway.'

'Keep your head up, shoulders back, but relaxed.' She was adjusting his posture when Ean walked in.

Clearly taken aback to find Rory there with Ailsa, all dressed up in his smart clothes, Ean's plan to talk to her was cast to the wind.

Ean blinked, taking in that Lyle was there too, and the ladies were clearly happy to have the men's company. He'd expected to see Cambeul at the bee night, but finding all three men in the heart of the bee threw him completely. He forced a smile.

'Ean!' Skye said cheerily, sensing the tension. 'Come away in. We're just practising for the show.'

'Would you like a cup of tea?' Ailsa offered him, feeling her heart react seeing him standing there in his kilt looking handsome but lost. Rory was by her side, unwilling to step back. She stepped forward.

'No, I just came in to tell you that the marquee has been booked for the fashion show event,' he said, looking at Ailsa, but including Skye and Holly.

'That's great,' Skye said, genuinely delighted.

'Thank you for organising that,' Ailsa told Ean.

Nodding, he smiled and started to head out. 'I'll let you get on with your rehearsals.'

The look he gave Ailsa as he saw her with Rory, before heading through to the front of the knitting shop, jolted her senses, but there was nothing she could do at that moment without causing a scene in front of everyone. So she smiled and continued to instruct Rory.

'When you're walking down the runway with, for instance, Holly, make sure you stay by her side. Don't walk ahead of her, or seem like you're tagging along. Exude pleasant confidence.'

Rory adjusted his expression. 'Like this?' His fabulous blue eyes glanced down at her and she could see the attraction in him, bubbling under the surface.

'Yes, and gaze out at the audience, rather than look down at the runway. Don't focus on any one person in the audience. Skim over everyone.'

Rory took in everything Ailsa was telling him.

Lyle straightened his shoulders and walked a few steps with Holly, trying to look at everyone but no one in particular.

'That's it, Lyle,' Ailsa said, acknowledging his effort.

But all the while, Ailsa kept thinking about Ean. Had he really come all the way down from the castle to tell them about the marquee? She doubted that. And the way he looked at her...

Ean drove away from the main street, along the harbour road, feeling himself in turmoil.

He glanced at the sea as he drove along. Far in the distance the waves were starting to rise and would soon be sweeping in to disturb the flat calm of the shore. A storm was on its way.

In that moment he changed his mind, slowed down, swung the car around on the quiet coastal road, and headed back with sheer determination to the knitting shop.

Pulling the car up outside the shop, he got out and walked with purpose straight through to the back room where the laughter and chatter still dominated the evening.

A lull descended on the gathering as everyone saw the tall kiltie standing there once again, this time looking like he was in no mood to be put off his stride.

Ailsa was beside Rory and Lyle, adjusting their stances for the runway modelling, and glanced round, wide–eyed when she saw that Ean was back.

'A word with you, Ailsa.' Ean's rich voice resonated in the momentary lull, and struck a chord right through her heart.

She nodded and followed him through to the front of the premises where they stood in relative privacy in the warm glow of the knitting shop.

Ailsa felt her heart racing and sensed the strength in him as he towered over her, gazing at her with those gorgeous green eyes.

'Have dinner with me the evening after the fashion show, Ailsa.' His voice resonated around her, causing her heart to react with excitement.

'Yes,' she heard herself say.

Ean nodded, polite, assured. 'Until then.' Without another word, he strode out of the shop, got into his car and drove off into the night, leaving her standing in a bubble of realisation. Had she just agreed to everything she'd secretly long wanted?

Walking back through to join the others, she felt herself still connected to Ean, thinking about him as he was no doubt thinking about her.

'That was fast,' Rosabel remarked to Ailsa. 'Did Ean have anything to say for himself?'

Ailsa nodded, but was still emerging from her own bubble of thoughts.

Skye stepped close to Ailsa, eyes wide with interest. 'What did Ean say?'

'Everything.' Ailsa's one word answer explained everything too.

Cambeul unwittingly broke the spell. 'The ladies have asked me to join them on the runway.'

Ailsa blinked. 'That's great.'

'I've never covered a show that I've participated in,' Cambeul said, looking happy to be part of it. 'Another first for this feature. I can't wait to tell Celia.'

As if on cue, Cambeul's phone rang. He picked up and spoke before she did, another first. 'I'm walking on the runway,' he announced. 'Skye and Holly want me to join in the show.'

Celia paused and considered, then decided she loved this idea. 'What are you wearing? A vintage suit?'

'They've asked me to wear a kilt. I can hire one here. The men are kilted to accompany the models. We're all going commando.'

Celia cut–in. 'Spare me the details. But send me preview pics of the dress rehearsal so I can envisage the feature. This puts another tilt on the slant I'd planned. But it's tilting in favour of a really exciting feature. This issue is going to be one of our jewels in this year's crown.'

'I'll do that,' Cambeul confirmed. 'I'm at the knitting bee night. We're rehearsing for the show and eating cake.'

'Don't have too much fun. Remember, you have to come back to the real world when the show's over,' Celia warned him.

For the first time since he'd arrived on the island, Cambeul realised that he wasn't looking forward to going back to the city. He'd felt the opposite on the way over on the ferry, wishing the feature was done and he was sailing home to Glasgow. But so much had happened in a compressed timescale of fun and forging new friendships.

'I may never come home,' Cambeul joked with Celia. He was joking, wasn't he? 'Oh, and, Skye says you're welcome to come over for the show.'

'Is she there?' Celia's clipped tone startled him.

'Eh, yes...' Cambeul handed his phone to Skye. 'Celia wants a word with you.'

Skye took the phone, but before she could utter a syllable, Celia's assured voice cut right through her.

'Skye! Keep an eye on Cambeul for me. Don't let his objectives deviate from why he's there, to write the feature and cover the fashion show.'

'I'll keep him right,' Skye assured her, unfazed by the editor's take charge attitude. And then she threw a curve ball back at her. 'Remember, you're welcome to come over for the fashion show.'

'I don't do ferries,' Celia replied.

'If you change your mind...'

'I won't, probably. Besides, Seona has been sussing out accommodation on the wildest chance that we would attend the show. She says the castle is fully booked, and so are the other small hotels.'

'You can stay with Holly and me at our house. We've plenty of room. We've invited Delphine from the fairytale tea dress shop in Edinburgh, and a few others to enjoy a sleepover after the show.'

Celia laughed. A genuine one. 'A sleepover? I didn't ever do those when I was of an age when silliness was appropriate.'

'A first time for that as well then,' said Skye. 'And I believe you have a liking for those.'

Celia smiled, liking Skye's pluck. Skye was a worker, and she pushed hard for what she wanted. 'No promises that I'll be at the show.'

'None taken, Celia. Nice to speak to you. I'll hand you back to Cambeul.'

'A sleepover!' Cambeul exclaimed, getting the first word in again.

'Not in a million years,' Celia hissed in his ear.

'There's a chance then,' he said.

Celia refused to be baited, and concluded with a comment to bring the conversation back to magazine business. 'Our rivals have wind of what we're up to. Watch out and stay sharp.'

'I'm keeping sharp. I was swimming in the sea this morning,' Cambeul told her.

'It's autumn.' She shivered at the thought of it.

'The water was fairly mild.'

'Fine, but keep me updated.' Celia clicked off, bringing the call to a close.

Everyone chattered and enjoyed another round of tea while practising for the show, and tried on the different dresses.

Rowen wore a fifties tea dress. She was in her thirties, very attractive, and made hand–spun yarn that she sold from home. Her long red hair shone in silky waves, and her green eyes and pale complexion suited the floral print dress. She was one of the knitting bee members that had taken part in Holly and Skye's fashion party recently at the castle, like a practise run for the fashion show.

'I'd like to wear vintage,' Rowen said to Skye and Holly. 'But what's the ideal way to get into wearing it? Not just party dresses like this, but for during the day. I'd feel that everyone was staring at me if I popped out to the grocers wearing a fifties tea dress.'

'That's something a lot of people ask us,' Holly explained. 'One of the easiest and economical ways to start wearing vintage as a regular part of your daily wardrobe is to start with a couple of skirts — a denim skirt and a tartan one.'

The women sipped their tea and shared the last of the cake with the men, and listened to Holly explain.

'What type of denim skirt?' said another member. 'I'd love to wear something like that.'

'Skye and I both have seventies denim skirts in our wardrobes,' Holly revealed. 'I have a light blue and a dark blue. The seventies denim skirts are wonderful.'

'What length are they?' yet another member wanted to know.

'Midi and maxi skirts. So mid–calf and a bit longer,' said Holly. 'The skirts are A–line, and I don't mean flared, just gently sweeping out rather than straight skirts. They're front button skirts which adds to the style and I find them very easy to wear.'

'Button through vintage denim skirts are so flattering,' Skye said, joining in the conversation. 'I'm the same as Holly. I have a light blue and dark indigo denim. Both seventies midi and maxi lengths. I wear mine summer and winter. They're so versatile. And real bargains.'

Rowen sounded enthusiastic. 'That's what I want. Vintage pieces that I can add to my everyday wardrobe.'

'It's what you wear with them that matters too,' Holly added. 'I wear a long sleeve cotton top or jumper in red, pastel shades of blue, pink and lemon, or white. The light blue denim works with most of these colours. The dark denim looks brilliant with red, white and bold tones.'

'You've really put me in the notion of finding a vintage denim skirt like that,' said Rowen. Several other ladies agreed.

'Holly's right about what to wear with them,' said Skye. 'I love white broderie anglaise blouses or tops for the summer. In the winter I team them with a cropped cardigan, like an Aran cable knit. Or a gorgeous blue or pastel double–knit cardigan. We're lucky we're knitters and can make our own cardigans from all the fabulous colours of yarn available.'

Elspeth, an expert knitter, nodded. 'I get so excited when the new yarns come into the shop. It's autumn, but I'm still loving the sky blue, sea blue and pastel pink yarns.'

'What about the tartan skirts?' Rowen said to Holly.

'Tartan vintage skirts are some of my favourite pieces,' said Holly. 'Skye and I both love tartan in red, blue and green tones. The length and the style are the same as the denim skirts. And the tops that work with the denim transfer well when worn with the tartan skirts.'

'We've even got Ailsa into wearing a tartan skirt,' Skye said, gesturing to the one Ailsa was wearing with the long sleeve, hand knitted red jumper.

Rowen and the ladies nodded, liking Ailsa's outfit.

'In the summer I wear comfy pumps with the skirts,' Holly told them. 'And I wear warm tights and boots for the winter.'

'Then you can add a couple of vintage dresses to your wardrobe,' said Skye. 'A classic tea dress or a shift dress. I wear mine with the cardigans, and I have two denim jackets, a light blue and dark blue, that are interchangeable with most things in my wardrobe. I've embroidered flowers and small motifs on the jackets to add to the designs.'

'Embroidering the denim...' Primrose said thoughtfully. 'I like that idea.'

'I'm going to buy myself denim and tartan skirts,' said Rosabel. 'I have cardigans I've knitted that would go with them. It'll be like a whole new wardrobe.'

Cambeul had been scribbling notes, listening to the conversation. 'Denim is a wardrobe staple, and I love the notion of wearing tartan skirts and dresses.'

Lyle and Rory finished their tea and cake.

Putting his cup down, Lyle directed his question at Cambeul. 'Any tips for menswear?'

'Classic.' Cambeul's one word summarised his advice. 'You can't go wrong with the classics. And I mean the crisp white shirts, pin stripe shirts, traditional ties, silk backed waistcoats, well–cut suits whether off–the–peg, made–to–measure or bespoke. Pre–loved designer or bespoke suits are great bargains. It's often worth paying to have slight alterations made to a vintage suit to make it fit perfectly.'

'What about kilts?' Rory said to Cambeul.

'They're in a class of their own, fortunately for us,' Cambeul replied.

'The perfect foil for the lovely ladies,' Rory concluded.

'Exactly. That's why we want to feature Scottish vintage fashion in the magazine,' said Cambeul.

'Ghillie shirt or white shirt and tie with my kilt?' Rory said to Cambeul, wanting his expert advice.

'Ah, now, that depends on the effect you want to create,' said Cambeul. 'I wrote a feature about this a while ago. The conclusion was that the ghillie shirt has a sex appeal, being open at the neck and laced up the front. A white shirt and tie is high class, usually teamed with a waistcoat and long or cropped jacket.' Cambeul glanced around at the ladies. 'What would you prefer Rory to wear, ladies? Ghillie shirt or shirt and tie?'

A show of hands made the ghillie shirt a clear winner.

'I hope the ghillie was going to be your choice for the fashion show,' Cambeul said to Rory.

'Aye, it was,' said Rory.

Lyle smiled. 'I may have to rethink my outfit.'

'No, wear what suits you,' Cambeul told Lyle. And then he joked. 'We can't all wear ghillie shirts to please the ladies, can we, Rory?'

Laughter and light–heartedness filled the room until the bee night finally came to a cheery close. Everyone filtered out of the knitting shop, waving to Morven and Elspeth. Ailsa and others had helped Skye and Holly carry the dresses back to their shop. They'd hung them up on the rails and then went back to the knitting shop to help tidy up the tea and cake dishes, and fold the chairs away in the store cupboard. Morven and Elspeth were never left to clear the knitting bee set up on their own, and with all of them lending a hand they made light work of it.

Skye and Holly stepped outside the knitting shop and sensed a change in the sea air. Storm clouds were threatening in the distance.

'Can I walk you ladies back to your dress shop?' Rory said to Holly and Skye. He was still buzzing with the excitement of the night.

Skye smiled sweetly. 'Our shop is right there, Rory.' She motioned to it a few steps away.

Rory squirmed at his faux pas. 'Silly me.'

'No, it was well meant,' Holly assured him.

Rory breathed in the fresh night air. 'I enjoyed myself tonight.'

'I did too,' said Lyle. 'We weren't sure what we were letting ourselves in for, but we had a grand time.'

'I'll email you copies of the photos I took of you tonight,' Skye promised them. She'd taken them while

Rory and Lyle learned how to work the runway. 'Seeing how you looked at first, and then the improvement in your posture should bolster you both, and make you less nervous about taking part in the show in front of an audience.'

'Great,' said Rory and gave Skye his private email address, as did Lyle.

Bidding them goodnight, Lyle got into his car to head to his parents' farmhouse near thistle loch, while Rory climbed into his van to drive home to his house in the middle of nowhere. Waving, the men drove off, both heading towards the forest road.

Several ladies were chatting outside the shop before heading home. A couple of them hugged their arms around themselves for warmth, as the autumn air had a colder bite to it. Storm clouds swept across the sky, stretching the full length of the coast, threatening a wild, rainy night.

Shuggie drove up to take Cambeul back to the castle.

'Can I give any of you ladies a lift?' Cambeul offered out of politeness.

Three of the women took him up on his offer and piled into the back of the taxi, leaving Cambeul to gently lift Fluffy and his blanket on to his lap as he sat in the front with Shuggie. He'd been kitten sitting again while Nettie attended the bee night.

'I'm not laughing,' Shuggie said to him, his shoulders shaking, holding in his guffaws.

Fluffy gave Cambeul an acknowledging meow and then settled down happily to snooze on the magazine journalist's lap as Shuggie drove off into the night.

CHAPTER TEN

The wind sweeping in from the sea blew a warning that a storm was on its way. Ailsa glanced round at the thunderous clouds as she unlocked the front door of her cottage. The twinkle lights shone a welcoming warmth, and she was looking forward to relaxing after the hectic day and evening at the bee. And to think about Ean's dinner date invitation.

She hadn't told anyone at the bee what Ean had said to her, not yet. His words...*Have dinner with me after the fashion show, Ailsa*...rewound in her mind, along with her one word reply of acceptance.

Her heart thundered like the approaching storm even now as she thought about the implications, the complications.

The wind whipped through her dark hair blowing it back from her face. She glanced at the sea, like rippling dark silver in the bay and the waves churning in the distance heading for the shore.

A storm was on its way tonight, but she felt as if the tides in her heart were changing in her favour, making her feel a mix of trepidation and temptation. A powerful blend to contend with when all her energies were needed to focus on the forthcoming fashion show and her craft business. The weeks she'd been away doing the modelling work were still fresh in her mind, and she hadn't found time to relax in her cottage and enjoy unwinding in her cosy home again.

So many things were bubbling under the surface and rising like the tides. A fashion show on the island was a first, something she hadn't anticipated, but she was determined to help her friends pull it off and make it the success it deserved to be after all their hard work and hopes.

Now, on top of that, Ean had made a bold move after they'd circled around each other for so long, often being apart. There was nothing standing in their way now except the show. A dress rehearsal was planned one afternoon soon at the castle, and she'd promised Holly and Skye she'd be there to help organise it. And she would. But surely she'd see Ean at the castle. She wondered if he'd say anything about their dinner date. So many things to consider.

She let the wild wind blow away her tension, and then went into her cottage and closed the door against the impending storm.

As usual, the cottage had retained the heat of the day and it always felt cosy coming home.

After putting the kettle on for tea, she went through and set up the living room to unwind with a bit of comforting crafting — knitting perhaps, or embroidery, or...as she checked her laptop for orders, seeing there were a few, she thought about the denim skirts information the ladies had been talking about at the bee.

A quick browse online showed that there were lots of lovely vintage denim skirts for sale, and she smiled when she saw that the one she liked best was available from Holly and Skye's shop. It was a real bargain, light denim, front button, and in great condition. She couldn't resist and pressed the buy button, picturing Holly and Skye smiling when they saw her order.

While checking the denim bargains online, she saw another few names she recognised including — Bee and Joyce, whose vintage fashion shop was in Glasgow. Bee worked at the shop as a dressmaker, and designed fabric and dress patterns. Joyce owned the shop, and they repaired pre–loved fashion, upscaled the designs and made their own vintage style dresses. A dress made from Bee's fabric was printed with pansies, tea roses and sunflowers. Ailsa had browsed through their shop when she was in Glasgow and loved their own creations as well as their authentic pre–loved pieces. She'd met them a few times on the modelling circuit and at craft fairs.

Living up to their reputation for selling beautiful dresses at great prices, Ailsa was reminded of the phrase — *champagne chic for lemonade money*. Looking great for less.

She was additionally reminded that vintage dress patterns were for sale, so she bought one that had a tea dress style with a couple of variations in the pattern to alter the sleeves and neckline. She had plenty of fabric in her stash including four metres of a rich rose floral print — roses on a light cream background — more than enough to make the dress. It had been a bargain buy and she'd loved the fabric and kept it in her stash for dressmaking.

Making dresses from vintage patterns was something that the ladies at the bee had done earlier in the year, and she'd joined in and made herself a floral print dress that had spring flowers in the design.

Dress necklines were a key feature in Ailsa's experience. Sweetheart necklines were classy and flattering, and she liked shawl collars too. Bows were pretty and added interest to a garment, and she was due to model a dress at the fashion show that had an illusion bodice neckline — a solid bodice with a sheer fabric overlay with sparkles that made it look like her shoulders and décolletage were sprinkled with starlight.

After making a cup of tea, she checked Esmie's website, another vintage fashion shop owner, and swooned at the velvet and satin dresses she had on sale.

Then she looked at Delphine's Fairytale Tea Dress Shop in Edinburgh and noticed that she still made and sold the little velvet evening bags. Ailsa owned one of these in burgundy, but always wanted another colour. The emerald velvet was nice, but an amber velvet for autumn was on offer. Sold. Ailsa now looked forward to receiving the autumn style bag. No wonder they were one of Delphine's most popular accessories. And her dresses were amazing. Delphine designed and made her own as well as selling original vintage.

It would be lovely to see Bee, Joyce, Esmie and Delphine at the fashion show. And she started to wonder if she should take Skye up on her offer of a sleepover.

Feeling the tiredness of the day kick in, she finished her tea and went to bed without having knitted a stitch, but she'd enjoyed browsing the websites and looking at the exquisite fashions.

The storm raged along the coast, and the sea looked wild and wonderful. Tucked up under her quilt, she gazed out the window at the rainy night and fell sound asleep.

Ean watched the storm from his balcony, unable to settle down to sleep. The warrior trees refused to bend to the wind, but everything else was blowing in the strong breeze gusting across the island. The air had a scent of fresh potential mixed with the greenery and the sea. Or maybe it was his own heart trying to bolster him now that he had a dinner date pending with Ailsa. He couldn't get her beautiful face with her trusting blue eyes gazing at him, with interest, amusement and kindness, out of his thoughts.

That's why he couldn't sleep. Not because of the storm raging past the castle that didn't budge and never had in his experience. The castle was a stronghold and even the turrets had withstood many an assault on them by the weather and remained as solid as they always had been.

He couldn't have wished to live in a better fortress on the island. The castle had a majesty and magical quality in itself.

But the one person casting a spell upon his heart was Ailsa.

Standing strong on the balcony, wearing only his silk pyjama bottoms, the fierce wind blew through his thick auburn hair, sweeping it back from his sculptured features. He felt the determination in him rise. The dress rehearsal for the fashion show was scheduled soon, in an afternoon, as the other evenings in the function room were busy with party nights and dining for guests. He was bound to encounter Ailsa during the rehearsal afternoon. Bide your time, he told himself. Don't squander the chance to do things right. A romantic dinner the night after the fashion show would be the ideal time to talk to her, to reveal the strength of his feelings for her, and to tell her she'd been in his heart now for quite some time.

'Rough night?' Finlay said to Ean.

Ean joined Finlay for breakfast and sat down at their private table the following morning in the far corner of the function room.

'The storm,' said Ean. It wasn't a complete lie. Ailsa caused ripples of turmoil in him that no storm could trounce.

The thunderstorm had moved on near the dawn, leaving the island refreshed and sparkling bright in the morning sunlight. But the air had lost its warmth, and now felt like a mild autumn day rather than summer.

Finlay reached for a slice of toast and buttered it as he viewed his brother, reading him well. 'How are things between you and Ailsa?' He bit into his toast and waited for Ean to explain.

'I've asked Ailsa to have dinner with me the evening after the fashion show.' Ean poured milk on his cereal and fruit.

'Progress.' Finlay sounded pleased.

Ean told him about turning up at the knitting bee the previous night.

Finlay frowned. 'Rory was there, and Lyle?'

'And Cambeul. I expected him but not the others, though obviously they're now part of the show.'

Finlay sipped his tea. 'Merrilees wants me to walk with her at the show's finale. I've agreed.'

'You're modelling at the show?' Ean sounded surprised.

Finlay fudged the issue. 'It's not really modelling. The men are only walking the ladies down the runway at the end of the fashion show. I'll be sitting out front enjoying the whole show, as will the other men who've agreed to take part in the finale.'

'How many men are taking part?'

'Several, but not enough to partner with all the ladies. Skye and Holly said it's fine. They just want a few men to bolster the finale, and now with Murdo, Shuggie and a couple of the farmers joining in, they'll have what they need.'

'Murdo and Shuggie!' Ean was taken aback.

'Shuggie is walking with his wife, Nettie,' Finlay explained.

Ean nodded. 'Ah, right. But Murdo?'

'He said Skye roped him in. You know what she's like.'

'Oh, yes.'

'But when I was talking to him last night, he seemed well up for it. And he's been partnered with one of the women — Geneen.'

'Geneen! I didn't know she was modelling,' said Ean.

'She's a member of the knitting bee and a lot of the ladies from the bee are modelling, including Rosabel and Primrose.'

'Does Innis know?'

'Do I know what?' Innis breezed in and sat down, helping himself to tea and toast.

'Rosabel and Primrose are modelling at the fashion show,' Ean told him.

'They never said anything to me. But I think I've got a reputation for disapproving of things.'

'Well earned,' said Finlay.

Innis went to defend the accusation, but then smirked. 'I'm working on being more...agreeable.'

'Skye's influence?' Finlay suggested.

Amber eyes glanced across the breakfast table at Finlay. A momentary spark, ready to become enflamed, and then dowsed. 'Why would I be influenced by Skye?'

'I think you know why.' Finlay's tone accompanied his words, doubling his meaning.

'I'm too busy with my cake shop and other business to get romantically involved with any young lady,' Innis said unconvincingly. 'Besides, I've known Skye for a while now. If I'd been thinking of dating her, I'd have done it by now.' He glanced at Ean. 'No offence. I know we're different. You'll find the right time to talk to Ailsa.'

'Ean has,' Finlay revealed before Ean had a chance.

Innis looked at Ean. 'Is that right?'

Ean nodded. 'I'll be the talk of the gossip this morning after storming into the knitting bee last night with more arrogance than I'd intended.'

'What did Ailsa say?' Innis was keen to know.

'Yes.' Ean didn't elaborate.

Innis frowned. 'Is that it?'

Ean nodded.

Innis smiled. 'You two are made for each other.'

They laughed, and the atmosphere lifted, and Ean felt relieved to have told his brothers his intention with Ailsa. They were bound to find out. The gossip would be rife today.

Finlay gave Ean a reassuring pat on the shoulder. 'Ailsa said yes. That's what matters. You probably took her aback being so bold marching into the bee night.'

'I think I took myself aback too,' Ean admitted. 'I couldn't get a wink of sleep last night, and not because of the storm.'

'The castle weathers storms well,' said Finlay. 'We're fortunate to live in such a stronghold. But it's the women in our lives that cause us unrest. I'm lucky I found Merrilees. I never expected her to walk into my life and now I couldn't be happier.'

'Folk often say I'll find romance when I least expect it,' said Innis. He looked thoughtful. 'They tend to say that the woman for me will arrive one day off the ferry.'

'Merrilees did,' Finlay confirmed. 'It was true for me.'

'I've known Ailsa for a wee while,' Ean said, 'but I made a mistake dating someone else. Now I'm seeing things clearer. And Ailsa has been away a lot to the mainland, as have I, and we move in different circles, so it's not as if I encountered her every day.'

Innis thought about the lovely young woman he encountered almost every day. He knew he hadn't engaged with her most times. Skye probably thought he was a moody and difficult man. And maybe he was. But could the woman for him have been coming into his shop, smiling cheerily to buy cakes? Each time he thought how often he'd brushed aside her smiles and barely acknowledged her, his heart felt ache and shame. And yet, despite this, Skye's lightness of character had continued to breeze into his shop, undeterred by his dour attitude.

'You thinking about Skye?' Finlay said to Innis.

'Maybe.' Innis didn't elaborate, and the protective shield rose up. He ate his breakfast, and they talked about the new guests due to arrive, and another wedding booked at the castle.

Skye phoned Ailsa. 'We're drowning in dress orders. Help!'

'I'm on my way.'

'Bring a water wheely with you,' Skye called jokingly. 'I haven't seen Holly since she submerged into a sea of taffeta and tulle.'

Ailsa laughed and hurried along from her craft shop.

CHAPTER ELEVEN

Ean wasn't the main topic of gossip because Ailsa hadn't told anyone that he'd asked her to have dinner. But Geneen was standing at the castle's reception booking in more guests, and smiled knowingly at Ean as he went past. She knew he'd walked into the bee and wanted to talk to Ailsa, but nothing more than that. In comparison to other gossip flying around that morning, this was tame.

Headlining the gossip was the forthcoming fashion show, with tickets now sold out. The local farmer supplying the marquee was being asked to supply two now as the overspill of guests grew.

'I'm heading down to the main street,' Ean told Geneen. 'I won't be long if anyone needs me.'

'Okay, Ean,' said Geneen, and continued to deal with the guest bookings.

Ean drove away from the castle and down to the post office to pick up a special delivery of spotlights for the show. Murdo was busy organising the stage and runway, without disruption to the guests, working diligently behind the scenes, so Ean said he'd pick up the delivery.

The amber glow of the sun striking the sea made the water look like liquid bronze, and the artist in him wished he'd time to spend the day painting it. He often painted outdoors and scenes like this were easier to capture in their true light. But he pulled the car over and snapped a few photos of it with the intention of painting it when the current rush of business settled down again.

Then it occurred to him... Once the fashion show rehearsal afternoon and the show itself were over, his life would hopefully be on a different path yet again. One with Ailsa in his life. Of course he'd have time to paint. But things would surely be different if they became a couple. His heart soared at the thought of this. Not long now until the rehearsal afternoon, and a chance to gauge whether Ailsa was still going to have dinner with him.

'I never thought we'd be this busy,' Holly said, packing up another dress order.

Skye scrolled through the online orders on the computer. 'We've nearly finished packing all of them.' And then she laughed. 'Ailsa!'

Ailsa carefully wrapped a velvet and brocade cocktail dress in tissue paper and handed it to Holly. They had a sort of production line going.

'I wondered when you'd finally see my order. I placed it last night. An impulse buy with all the talk of denim skirts. But I do want it,' Ailsa insisted.

Holly accepted the folded cocktail dress from Ailsa and wrapped it up ready for delivery to the post office. A load of packages were piled up on a table in the front shop.

'You've ordered one of our denim skirts?' Holly said, smiling. 'I wonder what gave you that idea?'

The three of them giggled.

'Pop through to the storeroom and help yourself to the skirt,' Skye told Ailsa.

'I'm buying the skirt,' Ailsa insisted.

'No you are not,' Holly countered.

'Away through and pick it up,' said Skye. 'It's yours. And thanks for coming over and helping us pack up all these orders.'

Ailsa finished folding a shift dress, and then excitedly hurried through and fished out the denim skirt from the storeroom. She came back clutching it, nodding with glee.

'Oh, yes, this is great,' Ailsa enthused, holding it up against herself to check the midi length. 'And I love the wee ladybird that's embroidered on it.'

'I embroidered it,' Skye told her. 'There was a mark on the front, from a blue ink pen, difficult to get out of the fabric, so I embroidered a ladybird instead of a strawberry or cherry that are my go–to favourites.'

'I love it all the more that you embroidered it, Skye,' said Ailsa.

Smiling that Ailsa was happy with her skirt, Skye lifted up a bundle of parcels. 'Right, I'm going to start loading these into the car to take them to the post office.'

Ailsa and Holly finished parcelling up the last two orders while Skye balanced a pile of the packages and carried outside to their car. Putting them in the boot, she turned to go back in for more and saw Innis sorting beautifully iced cakes in his window display. Usually she'd wave and smile, accustomed to a hit or miss reaction that he'd respond in kind, but something different happened that took her aback...

Innis waved to Skye first.

She blinked, thinking she'd been in such a fug of fashion packing that she'd misread him. But no, he smiled, a sexy smile that hit her heart with an unexpected shot of excitement. Lately, she'd relegated her feelings for Innis to the back burner. Now there he was smiling at her and looking so sexy handsome.

Skye smiled and waved back at him, and then went into the shop to collect the rest of the parcels.

'Innis just waved to me from his shop window — first,' Skye announced as she walked in.

Holly's eyes widened. 'Really?'

'Yes,' said Skye. 'Maybe he's been eating some of that delicious cake icing and it's sweetened him up.'

Ailsa looked thoughtful.

Holly picked up on the look. 'What? You're hiding something.'

Ailsa couldn't hide her news any longer and Ean's dinner invitation tumbled from her lips.

'Ean asked you to have dinner?' Skye sounded surprised. 'You minx! You never even hinted at that last night.'

Ailsa mumbled an apology. 'My brain was fried with everything from having Lyle and Rory turn up at the bee to learn how to walk like models, to Cambeul being part of our world now too. Then to top it off, Ean had a double dip run at me. First coming in and using the marquee news as an excuse for being there.'

Holly's expression lit up with realisation. 'When all the time he'd really wanted to ask you out on a date.'

'Seeing the throngs of men at the bee probably threw him for a loop,' said Skye.

Ailsa agreed. 'He really didn't say much more than to have dinner with him. I said yes. He said, *until then*. And that was it.'

'Men only act like that when they love you more than anything,' said Holly.

Ailsa felt herself blush. 'But surely, Ean doesn't...'

'Oh, I think he does,' said Skye.

While Skye drove off to the post office with the parcels, Holly went with Ailsa to her craft shop to help her pack her orders.

'Thanks for helping me, Holly.'

'We'll make short work of this.' Holly held up a shawl Ailsa had knitted. 'This is lovely work.'

'The shawls sell well and I like knitting them.'

The orders weren't as many as in the dress shop, but there were enough to keep them busy.

'You'll make it in time for the post office,' Holly said, helping Ailsa put the packages in the back of her car.

Waving to each other, Ailsa headed to the post office and Holly walked along to her shop. She passed by the pretty pink knitting shop and stopped to admire the new window display.

Elspeth saw Holly and came out to chat.

'I love the autumn colours of yarn in your display,' Holly enthused. 'And you've got knitted pumpkins. I adore knitting those.'

Elspeth smiled. 'And I've a wee stuffed squirrel softie.' She pointed to the squirrel made from scraps of autumn coloured cotton fabric and stuffed with yarn. Other softies the shop used for advertising their yarn included owls, bumblebees and a sheep. Customers snapped up the softies, resulting in Elspeth having to make them regularly as customers had come to expect them for sale. Elspeth enjoyed making them, so it worked out well for everyone.

'The autumn tones look wonderful with the pink shop,' said Holly. She peered in at a selection of the yarn piled up. 'Those colours and textures are amazing.'

'Rowen dropped them off today. They're her latest shades and textures,' Elspeth explained. 'Customers will be lucky to get any because my aunty and me want them all.'

Holly laughed. 'Skye and I are like that when we get a new delivery of dresses. We've got a hoard of them at home, and we're still reluctant to part with some of the dresses that arrive.'

'Have you made the final selection for the show yet?'

'Nearly. We're getting there. Merrilees is helping to write the commentary and we're constantly updating her of what we're showing. We'll know for sure when we have the dress rehearsal.'

'Will we all have to dress up to the nines?' said Elspeth.

'Nooo, it's a dry dress rehearsal. In other words, just to iron out the rundown of the event, pair the couples, advise on how the show will unfold, that sort of thing. We're not wearing the dresses. We'll do that on the night, and many of the bee members, like yourself, have already tried on the dresses they'll wear, or they're welcome to pop into the shop and do that.'

'I might pop in. I haven't selected an evening dress or one for that other category—'

'Champagne chic, lemonade money?'

'That's the one. Skye says it's glamour to the max.'

'Yes, we'll show the evening dresses, beautiful and classic is the theme for those,' Holly explained. 'Then we'll finish with the champagne numbers where anything goes as long as it's glitzy, glamorous and gorgeous.'

Elspeth's face lit up. 'It's so exciting.'

'Do you want to come in now? Fabulous dresses arrived today. They are amazing.'

'I'm just popping into the dress shop with Holly,' Elspeth called into Morven.

'Okay. If you don't come back in two days, I'll send out a search party,' her aunt joked.

Accompanying Holly into the shop, Elspeth tried on several dresses in a flurry of gold lamé, silver shimmer and ruby sequins.

'What do you think?' Elspeth said to Holly, too mesmerised to decide on two.

'The gold lamé looks like it was made for you and is perfect for the evening wear. But the champagne winner is the silver shimmer.'

This was the dress Elspeth was wearing. The long, mermaid tail fell like a waterfall of sequins, and the thirties era styling had a long scarf that was slung from the front of one shoulder and rippled down like a trail at the back.

Elspeth nodded. 'Sheer glamour. Could you take a picture so I can show Brodrick? There's no way I can explain this level of silver sensation.'

Holly used Elspeth's phone, took pictures in the shop, and then suggested she stand outside in the fading sunlight. The sequins scintillated and she captured the look on a short video too.

Elspeth gazed at the photos and video. 'Oh look at the back of the dress. It's as glamorous as the front,' she said, able to view it now. Elspeth's blonde hair shone like silk and the whole look was sheer glam.

Brodrick saw them from the window of his cafe bar and came out to talk to them, part joking but genuinely impressed. He was tall, strong, thirty–two, with dark russet hair and green eyes.

'What's going on here?' he said.

Elspeth explained.

'A fine choice for the fashion show,' Brodrick agreed.

'And my evening dress for the night is gold lamé,' Elspeth added.

'I don't know exactly what that is, but it sounds very glamorous,' he said, smiling with love in his eyes for Elspeth.

As they were talking, Skye drove back from the post office and parked outside the dress shop. Ailsa followed a moment or two later and pulled up at her craft shop.

'Elspeth has selected her dresses,' Holly explained. 'I was taking pictures.'

Ailsa joined them and admired the silver dress.

Elspeth then disappeared back into the dress shop with Holly to change out of the silver dress, and then they hurried outside again.

They all chatted for a few minutes, and then as the women agreed how hectic their days had been, Brodrick made an offer.

'Come in and have dinner.' He gestured to his cafe bar.

Elspeth usually had dinner with him, and was happy to have the others join them.

'It would save making dinner,' Skye admitted. 'I'm cream crackered.'

Brodrick laughed. 'Come in then and relax. I've new items on my autumn menu.'

Elspeth had already tried most of them. 'I can thoroughly recommend the autumn vegetable pie with mashed potatoes and neeps. The pastry is delicious and so is the gravy.'

'I know what I'm having,' Skye joked.

Ailsa wasn't sure if she was included and went to walk away to her craft shop.

'Where do you think you're going, Ailsa?' Brodrick said, smiling at her and beckoned all of them into the cafe bar.

The aroma of savoury dinners filled the air and the classic but welcoming decor was so inviting. Vintage prints of the island hung on the coffee and cream walls and enhanced the traditional, dark neutral tones of the decor. The shiny gold balustrades along the length of the bar were gleaming, and lights reflected in the mirror behind it. Staff tended to customers and it was pleasantly busy. The cafe bar included an ice cream counter with a great selection of flavours, like an ice cream parlour. Brodrick had kept the ice cream aspect of the original cafe when he'd taken it over a few years ago.

A table near the corner beside one of the front windows was reserved for Elspeth, with plenty of room around the table for all of them.

'Are you joining us?' Elspeth said to Brodrick.

'Nope, so you're free to gossip about me, or any other men you secretly fancy,' he said.

The women laughed.

As their dinner was served, they talked about the fashion show and about Ean, Rory and Innis.

'Ice cream, ladies?' Brodrick offered after their main course plates were cleared away by the waiting staff.

'Can we have one of your ice cream buffets please?' said Elspeth.

'Coming right up,' he said.

Every favourite flavour was included, along with wafers and cones to make pokey hats, allowing the ladies to enjoy samples of all the delicious recipes.

Brodrick approached their table when they'd finished their ice cream.

'While you're all here, ladies, can I ask...do I have to wear my kilt to the afternoon rehearsal at the castle?'

Holly spoke up. 'No, it's like a dry run without all the falderals.'

'I have a ticket for the show,' he said. 'Will I be able to sit in the audience and watch the show before I walk with Elspeth at the finale?'

'Yes,' said Skye. 'All the men will be in the audience during the show, and then pop backstage when we signal them, to walk on the runway for the final part of the fashions.'

'Great. That suits me. I'll be at the rehearsals. Do you have many men taking part?' he said.

'A fair few,' Holly told him. 'It started with you and Lyle, and now we've got Rory, Finlay, a couple of farmers, Shuggie, Murdo and Cambeul.'

'Cambeul — he's the magazine journalist,' said Brodrick.

'Yes, he's covering the show for a magazine feature,' Holly told him.

'Elspeth explained that I could be pictured in the magazine, and I'm fine with that, or in the video,' he said.

'I'm glad you're taking part,' said Skye. 'It gives a boost to the show's finale.'

'Apart from Finlay, are any of his brothers joining in?' Brodrick said to Skye.

'No, but we only need a few handsome and strapping men like yourself,' Skye confirmed.

Brodrick smiled, and then left them to enjoy relaxing with their tea.

'What should I do about hair and makeup?' Elspeth said to them.

'The call–sheet is clean clean,' Skye explained. 'Clean hair. No makeup. It's best to wash your hair in the morning so that it's freshly washed that day but more manageable by the evening.'

Elspeth understood. 'I'll do that.'

'We have a few ladies from the knitting bee with hair and makeup skills helping us on the night,' Holly added. 'Others will be backstage assisting us to get dressed and hanging the clothes in the order they'll be worn in. Rails are being set up backstage and we're taking the dresses there on rehearsal day and leaving them so there's no last minute scramble on the show day. Every dress will be labelled with the model's name and the running order it appears.'

'It sounds well organised,' Elspeth remarked.

'The three of us have taken part in numerous shows,' Skye added. 'We've never been part of organising them, but we've seen the things that can go haywire or throw a spanner in the works, and we're trying to make things run smoothly.'

'Nothing will go entirely to plan,' said Holly. 'There will be the inevitable chaos and ructions, but hopefully we can avoid most of these.'

Skye sighed. 'But we all know what things are like on the island. If you want a quiet life, go and live in a city on the mainland.'

The others laughed and agreed.

'It's a full and hectic life on the island,' Elspeth agreed. 'I had a quieter time living in Glasgow.'

'Then you'll know exactly what I mean,' said Skye.

Elspeth nodded, and she was starting to feel the sense of fun increase, especially as she'd have Brodrick there walking with her at the end of the show. This was something for the archives, she thought. Happy memories for Brodrick and her to look back on.

After chatting and having another round of tea, they all headed home, agreeing to do their best at the forthcoming rehearsals.

Ailsa arrived back at her cottage, feeling the change of season in the air. It had been another hectic day, but the time was flying by and soon it would be the afternoon rehearsal at the castle, and a possible encounter with Ean.

Secretly, she would've liked to walk down the runway accompanied by Ean, but he obviously didn't want to do that. They'd yet to decide the man she'd be partnered with. She really didn't mind. The show was about fun and fashion. And she aimed to enjoy it.

CHAPTER TWELVE

'Ean's in his room having tea and crumpet,' Murdo told Ailsa, Holly and Skye.

Conspicuous by his absence at the dress rehearsal, they'd finally asked Murdo where Ean was.

Hiding in his room was the truth, in part, although he did have an important piece of business to attend to. A wedding planner wanted to know the details of the castle's facilities and needed a prompt response. The task had fallen, as it often did, to Ean, as he was adept at negotiating these sort of deals in a pleasant but efficient way that usually resulted in a wedding booking being made at the castle.

He could've replied later, but it was a handy excuse to avoid being in the furore of the fashion rehearsals. To his credit, Murdo had informed him that the rehearsals were going well, and that the ladies had everything in hand. Well, almost everything. Ean not being there upset the balance of what they'd expected. Even Innis was there, and as Rosabel and Primrose were there too, he'd closed the cake shop for the afternoon and put a notice in the window stating they were only open for the half day and would reopen the next morning. With such an effort from Innis, and Finlay taking charge of various other aspects, Ean was letting the side down slightly.

Murdo clarified what he'd said, gesturing to the afternoon tea spread the castle had laid on buffet–style along one side of the function room.

'Chef's outdone himself keeping in the vintage afternoon tea theme,' Murdo explained. 'A tray of tea and buttered crumpets were taken upstairs to Ean. He's hoping to join you a wee bit later.'

With the busy atmosphere, there was little time to dwell on this, and as the explanation satisfied their curiosity, the women got on with the task in hand — dealing with the rehearsals.

Skye and Holly were armed with clipboards and pencils, jotting down the running order and altering it when needed. Ailsa's advice was sought continually, and together they made short work of organising the dresses, the rundown and the models.

The afternoon dress rehearsal was taking place the day before the following night's fashion show.

This allowed Murdo and those helping him, including Rory, to assemble the runway solidly for the practise run and to keep it intact for the forthcoming evening's show.

'Everyone is mucking in,' Murdo told the women. 'It's heartening to see all the willing hands.'

It was indeed, and Skye and Holly, along with Ailsa, were confident that the show had the potential to run quite smoothly, while having a high ratio of excitement. The perfect blend of fashion and entertainment.

'We still need to allocate the remainder of the men to the models,' said Skye, checking her list.

'I'd like to see how the two farmers walk on the runway before we partner them up with the ladies,' said Holly.

Skye and Ailsa agreed.

'I'll get them up on the runway,' Ailsa offered, and went over to the two men.

'Can I ask you both to walk down the runway,' Ailsa said to them.

'What do we have to do?' one of them said to her.

'Nothing special. It's just so we can see who you'll suit to be partnered with,' she told him.

'Okay,' he said. And then the two of them were ushered to the start of the runway on the stage.

'Walk at a calm pace,' Ailsa told them from the dance floor level. 'One at a time. When you get to the end of the runway, pause for a second, and then turn to your right and walk back along and on to the stage.'

Nodding that they understood, the men went for it, both doing exactly what they were asked to do.

'Perfect,' said Ailsa. 'Now have a cup of tea and cake, and we'll let you know shortly the model you'll be teamed with.'

Happy with their performance, and muttering that it was a lot easier than they thought, the farmers went over to have their tea.

As they partnered them with a couple of the dressmakers from the knitting bee, another farmer walked in and approached Holly and Skye.

'Isn't that the farmer who fancies Rosabel,' Holly whispered to Skye.

'Yes, Rosabel told me he plies her and Primrose with bags of new tatties every season,' Skye whispered back.

'But Rosabel secretly likes him, doesn't she?' Holly added.

'I think so,' said Skye. 'We don't have anyone to partner Primrose and Rosabel yet.' She checked her notes. 'He could be ideal.'

'I'm a friend of Rosabel,' he said by way of introduction. 'And Primrose.'

'Yes, we were thinking of asking you to walk Rosabel down the runway,' said Holly. 'Would that be okay with you?'

His face lit up with joy. 'Definitely. I'm up for that.'

'Can you give us a demonstration of your walking style,' Holly said to him.

Without needing coaxing, the strapping and mature but good looking farmer took to the stage, walked strong and calm, turned to the right, and completed his walk back on to the stage.

'Wonderful,' Holly told him. 'You will walk with Rosabel for the show's finale. Help yourself to the buffet while we tell her.'

As he walked away, Rosabel and Primrose came hurrying over.

'We've partnered you with your farmer,' Holly said to Rosabel.

She looked delighted. 'He's not my farmer.' She started to blush. 'But he's looking very smart today. I've never seen him so well turned out. He's obviously made an effort, so okay, I'll walk with him.'

Skye ticked her list.

Not realising the farmer had headed back over to talk to them, Primrose blurted out a loud comment. 'I wonder if he's got a brother for me.' She giggled and then stopped as he spoke over her shoulder.

'No brother, but I brought my cousin with me.' He beckoned a mature man, not unlike himself, to come over.

'This is my cousin,' the farmer said.

The man was tall and as strapping as the farmer. 'Hello, girls,' he said, smiling politely.

Primrose cast Rosabel a look that said — oh yes, we're keeping him.

Skye took his name, asked him to walk, and then tick boxed another couple well paired.

Behind them, a man, large in height and stature, wearing a kilt that his strong build really suited, stood in the doorway of the function room, looking like he could fill it. But he looked a bit lost, so Skye approached him.

'Can I help you?'

'Murdo said you needed men to make up the numbers,' he said in a voice that resonated with strength. 'So I'm here to volunteer.'

'Wonderful!' Skye smiled. 'We're asking each man to walk down the runway so we can see his posture and style. Then we'll pair you with one of the models. Okay?'

'Eh, yes, that's okay with me. Where do I go?'

'Up on to the stage.' Skye explained what he had to do.

At first he looked perplexed, and then when Skye, Holly, Ailsa and a few other ladies clapped and cheered him on, sensing his nervousness, his confidence emerged making him look like a perfect, big, strong kiltie.

When he jumped off the stage unexpectedly, rather than using the steps, Skye suggested they team him with one of the ladies from the bee, and the two of them were introduced. The last that Skye and the others saw him, he was pouring the woman a cup of tea and they were chatting happily.

Murdo came rushing over to Skye, Holly and Ailsa. 'What's Big Rab up to?'

Skye blinked. 'You know him?'

'Aye! I asked him to come and help with the lifting and shifting backstage,' said Murdo. 'He's built like an ox. I wanted him to help us secure the stage and runway, not strut down it.'

The women laughed.

'Well, he's happy to walk for us,' said Holly.

Murdo laughed and hurried away.

Skye and Ailsa went over to the buffet for tea while chatting about pairing up the couples. Holly continued to show the models how to improve their posture.

Skye checked her list. 'We have Merrilees with Finlay, Elspeth with Brodrick, Nettie and Shuggie, Morven with her boyfriend Donall, Geneen and Murdo...'

Ailsa read the list too.

'So that leaves Lyle, Rory and Cambeul without a match,' said Skye.

'And you, me, Holly and Rowen,' added Ailsa.

Hearing their names mentioned the three men in question came over to join Skye and Ailsa.

The women discussed their plan. Skye scribbled the remaining name pairings on her list.

'Okay,' Skye announced to the men. 'We're pairing Rory with Ailsa...'

Rory smiled, delighted.

Unknown to them Ean had joined them and watched from the doorway of the function room, mentally kicking himself that he'd allowed Rory to be with Ailsa. He should've volunteered to be part of the show.

Skye continued, '...and Rowen with Lyle...'

Lyle's face lit up with a hundred sunbeams. Rowen smiled over at him, pleased to be partnered with him.

Skye concluded, '...and last but not least, we thought that Cambeul would make a great pairing with Holly.'

Both Cambeul and Holly were happy with this selection.

Skye shrugged. 'That leaves me to walk down on my own. But that's okay.'

Ailsa frowned. 'Are you sure?'

'Maybe I can double up,' Rory offered. 'I'll walk with Ailsa and then with Skye.'

A man's voice sounded strong and assured from the far side of the function room as he announced, 'I'll walk Skye down the aisle.'

The chatter stopped in that instant, and everyone looked round at Innis.

'Walk Skye down the runway,' Finlay corrected him, realising everyone took Innis' comment the wrong way. Or had they?

Innis' inner turmoil was hard to suppress, but he held strong. 'Yes, that's what I meant.'

Skye was lost for words and looked at Holly and Ailsa. A slip of the tongue from Innis, or a lot more than that? She wasn't sure.

Nodding firmly, Innis excused himself and walked away, heading upstairs to his suite.

The chatter resumed, but included whispers about Innis' faux pas.

'I guess Innis likes Skye,' one of the women whispered to her friends.

'Will I play the music samples for the show?' said Murdo.

'Yes, thank you,' Holly told him.

While Murdo went backstage, Ean approached Ailsa, Skye and Holly.

'Everything going well?' he said, trying to sound chipper while wishing he could rewind time and be the man partnered with Ailsa.

'Very well,' Holly told him.

Ean smiled tightly.

'Murdo said you were busy with castle business,' Ailsa told Ean.

'I was. Unexpected business, or I would've been here sooner,' he said, his voice tinged with turmoil.

'Ailsa, can you help us with our turns?' Nettie and Geneen called over to her. She'd shown them at the knitting bee, but they needed prompted again.

She smiled lightly at Ean, feeling her heart ache just looking at him.

Ean knew he'd messed up on the chance to have talked to Ailsa before their dinner date. Now, with the fashion show on the horizon tomorrow night, he'd have to bide his time to talk to her.

Innis had disappeared and not come back. No one, especially Skye, expected him to. He'd volunteered to partner with her at the show, but if he didn't fulfil his promise, she'd go it alone.

Overall, the dress rehearsal had been a resounding success.

'If the show goes half as well, it'll be a success,' Holly said to Skye.

Skye agreed, but in the back of her mind was Innis' comment.

Ailsa felt like her head barely touched the pillow that evening, and suddenly now it was the day of the fashion show. To say that it was a blur of excitement undervalued the potency of the atmosphere on the island. So many of the local residents were involved in it. Everyone from those modelling, to helping behind the scenes, part of the audience or the castle's staff working hard to keep the catering in line. Two marquees were erected in the vast gardens in front of the castle, and Murdo's stash of twinkle lights adorned both of them.

Cambeul had hired a kilt and practised his turns on the carpeted hallway of the castle. He'd gone commando, but wanted to make sure his pleats didn't reveal too much when he was walking with Holly. He'd written large chunks of the feature for the magazine. Now all he had to write was the actual show. He was confident he could do that. Covering fashion shows and events was his forte.

He'd been given a front row seat so he had a prime view, and there were six empty seats beside him. They weren't empty for long as Delphine, Esmie, Bee and Joyce were seated. All of them had worn vintage dresses in support of the show's theme. The two remaining seats were marked for Celia and Seona. Celia still hadn't confirmed if she did ferries yet.

Finlay spoke in confidence to Ean. 'It's not as if Rory is dating Ailsa. He's modelling with her.'

Ean felt even worse as the enormous turnout for the event filled the castle's function room and the marquees. Guests wanted to see the show, and staff had asked if they could pop through and have a peek from time to time while they were on duty. Ean and Finlay agreed that the staff were welcome to take a look.

Innis joined him, dressed to impress in his full kilt attire, as were Ean and Finlay. The three, fine and handsome brothers were the talk of the evening as the show was about to start. A hint of engagement gossip circulated as people speculated whether Finlay would soon ask Merrilees to marry him. He neither denied or confirmed the gossip.

Further rumours circulated, most getting the wrong end of the stick, about Rory stepping in to take Ailsa away from Ean. Then there was the gossip about Innis' comment regarding Skye.

Nettie and Morven, dressed in tasteful sequins and sparkle, sat up on the side of the stage ready to read the commentary. A sound system was already installed on the stage, so no extra set up was needed for this.

Shuggie sat in the audience beside Donall, both there looking proud at their ladies. Nearby, Brodrick,

Lyle and Rory watched as the lights dimmed and the show began...

The two empty seats beside Cambeul were now filled with Celia and Seona. Celia, looking every inch the fashion editor, sat coiffed and wearing a designer skirt suit in heliotrope heather pink. Even as the lights dimmed, Celia glowed like a hot pink beacon. Seona wore a designer dress in the season's latest autumn colours, thankful for the rail of dresses hanging in Celia's office from photo–shoots.

Ean, Finlay and Innis were seated in a front row opposite them.

Murdo had outdone himself again with the stage lighting and twinkle lights illuminating the stage while not distracting from the fashions as the models took to the runway.

Skye led the charge, followed by Ailsa, Elspeth, Merrilees, Rowen, Rosabel and Primrose, all wearing classic thirties dresses. Holly ended that fashion round wearing an art deco dress in sea green satin, with a fishtail hemline that trailed behind her as she disappeared backstage again.

A round of applause rippled through the audience.

'This is very professionally done,' Celia commented to Cambeul and Seona.

'The atmosphere is electric,' said Cambeul, taking notes.

The man hired to film the show kept to the unobtrusive shadows while capturing every moment.

Next up was a flurry of day dresses from the twenties to the seventies. Colourful, eclectic, light and airy, the models breezed down the runway, entertaining the audience with their splendour and style. Rosabel and Primrose wore their signature shades of pink and yellow, and those familiar with them, knowing they dressed in those colours while working at the cake shop, gave an extra cheer for their efforts.

The music changed to suit the mood of the eras, and the audience was taken aback when the sixties era hit them full force with everything from psychedelic shift dresses and minis worn with knee–length white boots. These were modelled by Skye, Holly, Ailsa, Elspeth, Rowen and Merrilees, while Rosabel and Primrose, along with several other ladies followed the display of sixties sensations with seventies colourful, full–length kaftans in strikingly bold patterns. Seventies denim then dominated the runway, showing how versatile and evergreen denim was.

Nettie and Morven's commentary added to the atmosphere:

The classic rose print fabric enhances the fit and flare design of Ailsa's dress.

Skye stands out from the crowd in this ruby red dress with kick pleats.

Geneen dazzles in dress sequins and diamante.

Rosabel wears a pink chiffon party dress suitable for every season.

Primrose's yellow drop–waist dress has a flattering scalloped neckline.

A clean silhouette shift dress is always in style. Elspeth wears it in burgundy velvet.

Merrilees' timeless blue A–line dress spans the decades and is bang up to date with today's fashions.

'This fashion show is sensational,' Celia whispered to Cambeul and Seona. 'It's a complete non–stop assault on the senses, and transcends the eras with fashions I'd long forgotten.'

Cambeul wrote this down. 'I'll quote you on that, Celia.'

'I'm glad they're filming this, because I want to watch it on a loop for style tips and inspiration,' said Seona.

Celia nodded. 'Make sure we get a copy of it. We'll put it on our website. This is going to totally soar.'

'Oh. My. Goodness!' Cambeul exclaimed as the tartan fashions started to fill the runway.

Holly opened with a full–length blue tartan silk and chiffon extravaganza, sweeping down the runway, looking like she belonged in a Scottish fairytale.

An array of tartan dresses from traditional to sensational were modelled by all the women. Everyone wore tartan dresses, and Scottish vintage designs, and even then, Skye, Holly and Ailsa made quick changes backstage, used to doing this, and emerged again with another number to model for the audience.

'I'm definitely wearing tartan for the new season,' said Celia, amid the cheering of the audience.

Ailsa concluded the tartan fashions wearing an outstanding taffeta tartan ball gown, created decades ago for a Scottish New Year party.

From tartan to evening dresses, the change of mood ignited further applause.

Ean, Finlay and Innis cheered and applauded too.

Ean's heart ached every time Ailsa appeared, looking beautiful in everything she wore.

Finlay's heart filled with excitement watching Merrilees. She wasn't a trained model like some of the others, but she was matching them in the modelling stakes and he couldn't have been more in admiration of her.

Innis saw the beauty in Skye, and more than that. She had a light to her, as if her character shone through too. That wonderful smile, a beautiful face and figure and long, strawberry blonde hair.

Brodrick was in awe of Elspeth and smiled at her as she searched the faces in the audience for him.

Rory noticed the looks exchanged between Ailsa and Ean and decided not to make a play for her tonight. She only had eyes for one man in the audience and it wasn't him. He cheered her on regardless, and the other ladies.

Lyle didn't noticed Rory's reaction. He was too busy enjoying the show and looking forward to accompanying Rowen.

The evening dresses were elegance and class personified, carefully selected to add impact to the finale.

Backstage was a flurry of activity as sequin cocktail party dresses were put on, glittering numbers, and dresses that exuded glamour to the max.

Morven and Nettie stood up from their commentary chairs and walked backstage to partner with Donall and Shuggie.

'Are all you ladies decent?' Murdo shouted through to them, as he lined the men up ready to head backstage to partner up with the ladies.

'Yes,' Holly shouted to him.

The men hurried in as the music changed to an upbeat vibe, and without wasting time, the first couple, Skye and Innis, walked on stage.

'You look beautiful,' Innis said to her, striding down the runway beside her.

Skye smiled up at him, and felt this was a moment she'd remember forever. Her dress was gold, full-length, enhancing her lovely slender but shapely figure. Her long hair fell in waves around her shoulders, and the cheers from the audience filled her heart with joy. As did Innis. *I'll walk Skye down the aisle.* His words still circled in her thoughts, but she pushed them aside. If Innis wanted to be with her, he was bold enough to tell her. Ean held back, but she'd a feeling that this wasn't the wolf's style. So she would wait to see if anything came of his comment. And wait to see how she felt about him. She was going to be busy. The show was electric. The success of it was about to take Holly and her, and their vintage dress shop, to another level. She wasn't sure where that would lead, but she planned to take every opportunity afforded them.

Finlay and Innis had grabbed Ean with them when they'd headed backstage.

'I'm not on the list,' Ean said to them.

'You don't need to be,' Finlay told him firmly.

Rory saw Ean and nodded to him, and then stepped beside one of the other women who didn't have a partner. She was delighted and walked down the runway with Rory.

This left Ailsa without a partner. She glanced at Ean and smiled.

Stepping out on to the stage, Ean went with her. Following them was Finlay and Merrilees.

Cambeul was in his element walking beside Holly and was already planning what to write for the feature about the modelling experience.

Elspeth's silver shimmer dress looked sensational as she was accompanied by Brodrick.

Nettie and Shuggie put on a happy show, with Nettie's dress sparkling under the stage lighting. The castle's receptionist was kitten sitting for them. Fluffy was sleeping behind the counter, tucked up in his basket and blanket.

Morven's satin and sequin dress shone under the lights as she walked with Donall.

Big Rab walked strongly with one of the women from the knitting bee, delighted to be on the arm of the big kiltie.

'I'm enjoying this more than I imagined,' Murdo said to Geneen, strutting beside her. 'And you're looking lovely in your sparkly dress.'

'Thank you, Murdo. You've worked hard to make the show go well,' said Geneen.

Holly and Skye stood front of stage and walked down together wearing fairytale vintage dresses and were cheered by the audience and participants alike.

Celia was the first to stand up and applaud them, causing a standing ovation in the crowd.

Delphine, Esmie, Bee and Joyce all stood and cheered their friends.

Walking back up to join the others, Holly and Skye waved to the audience.

Standing all together on stage, Ailsa glanced at Ean. He smiled at her, and leaned close. 'You look gorgeous,' he whispered.

Ailsa smiled at him, and then waved out to the cheering audience again.

As the show came to a crescendo of fashion, passion, music, glamour, romance and excitement, the applause and cheers from the audience and everyone involved filled the function room.

A spectacular night to remember was had by all.

Wearing a beautiful vintage dress with an illusion bodice neckline — a solid bodice with a sheer fabric overlay with sparkles that made it look like her shoulders and décolletage were sprinkled with starlight, Ailsa walked with Ean outside to one of the marquees.

The other guests filtered out from the show to the marquees. But Ean gently led Ailsa aside for a romantic moonlight walk in the castle's garden. The fairytale castle glowed behind them, and the music and chatter filtered out into the calm night air.

'Will you still have dinner with me tomorrow night at the castle?' Ean said to her.

'Yes, I'd love to.'

Ean pulled her close, wrapped her in his arms and kissed her lovingly. Ailsa felt her world tilt, feeling she was where she belonged with the man for her.

They then walked up to the marquees to join the others and enjoy the buffet and party night.

At the end of the wonderful evening, Ailsa headed home to her cosy cottage, her head and heart filled with love. She was looking forward to her dinner date with Ean at the castle the following night.

Tucked up in bed gazing out at the silvery sea, she went to sleep with thoughts of the perfect ending to the evening she'd enjoyed walking hand in hand in the moonlight with Ean, such a handsome man.

'I don't do jim–jams,' Celia told Skye at the sleepover. 'I brought my silk chiffon negligee with me.' She held up the garment. Celia's collar and cuffs were satin trimmed.

Skye shook her head. 'You can't run round the house playing chase in that or do bouncies on the bed.'

'A few of my worn out ex–boyfriends would beg to differ,' Celia said with a wicked smile.

'Celia!' Seona exclaimed.

And then they all burst out laughing.

The lights glowed like beacons from all the windows of Holly and Skye's parents' house until the dawn rose over the sea. The sleepover was enjoyed by all the ladies and new friendships formed amid the giggles and light–hearted fun.

The following morning, Holly and Skye, along with Ailsa, waved to Celia, Cambeul and Seona as they sailed off on the ferry back to Glasgow. Cambeul's editorial for the feature sounded wonderful from the descriptions he'd read to them, and they all agreed to keep in touch to make the feature in the magazine a success.

Delphine, Esmie, Bee and Joyce stayed for lunch before catching the late afternoon ferry back to the mainland. Holly and Skye thanked them for coming over to support them.

Later, in the evening, Ailsa walked into the castle wearing a vintage cocktail–length dress in champagne chiffon and silk shot through with sparkle.

Geneen welcomed her at reception. 'Ean's expecting you.'

At that moment, Ean came down the private staircase wearing a classic dark suit, waistcoat, white shirt and silk tie looking the most handsome she'd seen him.

'You look beautiful, Ailsa,' he said, taking her hand and leading her upstairs to his suite where a candlelit dinner for two had been set up on his balcony overlooking the castle garden where they'd had their kiss the night before.

As dinner was served, Ailsa smiled at him and gazed out at the starlit view. 'This is wonderful, Ean.'

He took a steadying breath. 'I have to tell you that these past months I've thought about you almost constantly. When you were away on the mainland I was looking forward to you coming back each time. I've loved you for a long time, and moments when we've met have given my heart hope that there was a chance for us to be together. I hope you feel the same way.'

'I do. I think we both want a happy life on the island,' she said, smiling at him.

'Yes, that's what I want,' he assured her.

Ean leaned across and kissed her, sealing the start of their romance in the wonderful fairytale castle on the island.

End

About the Author:

De-ann Black is a bestselling author, scriptwriter and former newspaper journalist. She has over 100 books published. Romance, thrillers, espionage novels, action adventure. And children's books (non-fiction rocket science books and children's fiction). She became an Amazon All-Star author in 2014 and 2015.

She previously worked as a full-time newspaper journalist for several years. She had her own weekly columns in the press. This included being a motoring correspondent where she got to test drive cars every week for the press for three years.

Before being asked to work for the press, De-ann worked in magazine editorial writing everything from fashion features to social news. She was the marketing editor of a glossy magazine.

She is also a professional artist and illustrator. Embroidery design, fabric design, dressmaking, sewing, knitting and fashion are part of her work.

Additionally, De-ann has always been interested in fitness, and was a fitness and bodybuilding champion, 100 metre runner and mountaineer. As a former N.A.B.B.A. Miss Scotland, she had a weekly fitness show on the radio that ran for over three years.

De-ann trained in Shukokai karate, boxing, kickboxing, Dayan Qigong and Jiu Jitsu. She is currently based in Scotland.

Her 16 colouring books are available in paperback, including her latest Summer Nature Colouring Book and Flower Nature Colouring Book.

Her latest embroidery pattern books include: Floral Garden Embroidery Patterns, Christmas & Winter Embroidery Patterns, Floral Spring Embroidery Patterns and Sea Theme Embroidery Patterns.

Website: Find out more at: www.de-annblack.com

Fabric, Wallpaper & Home Decor Collections:
De-ann's fabric designs and wallpaper collections, and home decor items, including her popular Scottish Garden Thistles patterns, are available from Spoonflower.
www.de-annblack.com/spoonflower

Also by De-ann Black (Romance, Action/Thrillers & Children's books). See her Amazon Author page or website for further details about her books, screenplays, illustrations, art, fabric designs and embroidery patterns.

Amazon Author page:
www.De-annBlack.com/Amazon

Romance books:

The Cure for Love Romance series:
1. The Cure for Love
2. The Cure for Love at Christmas

Scottish Highlands & Island Romance series:
1. Scottish Island Knitting Bee
2. Scottish Island Fairytale Castle
3. Vintage Dress Shop on the Island
4. Fairytale Christmas on the Island

Scottish Loch Romance series:
1. Sewing & Mending Cottage
2. Scottish Loch Summer Romance

Quilting Bee & Tea Shop series:
1. The Quilting Bee
2. The Tea Shop by the Sea
3. Embroidery Cottage
4. Knitting Shop by the Sea
5. Christmas Weddings

Sewing, Crafts & Quilting series:
1. The Sewing Bee
2. The Sewing Shop
3. Knitting Cottage (Scottish Highland romance)
4. Scottish Highlands Christmas Wedding
(Embroidery, Knitting, Dressmaking & Textile Art)

Cottages, Cakes & Crafts series:
1. The Flower Hunter's Cottage
2. The Sewing Bee by the Sea
3. The Beemaster's Cottage
4. The Chocolatier's Cottage
5. The Bookshop by the Seaside
6. The Dressmaker's Cottage

Scottish Chateau, Colouring & Crafts series:
1. Christmas Cake Chateau
2. Colouring Book Cottage

Snow Bells Haven series:
1. Snow Bells Christmas
2. Snow Bells Wedding

Summer Sewing Bee

Sewing, Knitting & Baking series:
1. The Tea Shop
2. The Sewing Bee & Afternoon Tea
3. The Christmas Knitting Bee
4. Champagne Chic Lemonade Money
5. The Vintage Sewing & Knitting Bee

The Tea Shop & Tearoom series:
1. The Christmas Tea Shop & Bakery
2. The Christmas Chocolatier
3. The Chocolate Cake Shop in New York at Christmas
4. The Bakery by the Seaside
5. Shed in the City

Tea Dress Shop series:
1. The Tea Dress Shop At Christmas
2. The Fairytale Tea Dress Shop In Edinburgh
3. The Vintage Tea Dress Shop In Summer

Christmas Romance series:
1. Christmas Romance in Paris
2. Christmas Romance in Scotland

Oops! I'm the Paparazzi series:
1. Oops! I'm the Paparazzi
2. Oops! I'm Up To Mischief
3. Oops! I'm the Paparazzi, Again

The Bitch-Proof Suit series:
1. The Bitch-Proof Suit
2. The Bitch-Proof Romance
3. The Bitch-Proof Bride
4. The Bitch-Proof Wedding

Heather Park: Regency Romance
Dublin Girl
Why Are All The Good Guys Total Monsters?
I'm Holding Out For A Vampire Boyfriend

Action/Thriller books:

Knight in Miami
Agency Agenda
Love Him Forever
Someone Worse

Electric Shadows
The Strife Of Riley
Shadows Of Murder
Cast a Dark Shadow

Children's books:

Faeriefied
Secondhand Spooks
Poison-Wynd

Wormhole Wynd
Science Fashion
School For Aliens

Colouring books:

Summer Nature
Flower Nature
Summer Garden
Spring Garden
Autumn Garden
Sea Dream
Festive Christmas
Christmas Garden
Christmas Theme

Flower Bee
Wild Garden
Faerie Garden Spring
Flower Hunter
Stargazer Space
Bee Garden
Scottish Garden
Seasons

Embroidery Design books:

Sea Theme Embroidery Patterns
Floral Garden Embroidery Patterns
Christmas & Winter Embroidery Patterns
Floral Spring Embroidery Patterns
Floral Nature Embroidery Designs
Scottish Garden Embroidery Designs

Printed in Great Britain
by Amazon